# All Were Wounded, None Were Lost

*A story of the two thousand stripling warriors.*

CURTIS ERCANBRACK

NEWMAN SPRINGS PUBLISHING
320 Broad Street
Red Bank, NJ 07701

First originally published by Newman Springs Publishing 2020

ISBN 978-1-63692-113-6 (Paperback)
ISBN 978-1-63692-114-3 (Hardcover)
ISBN 978-1-63692-115-0 (Digital)

Printed in the United States of America

To Jan, my wife; my wonderful family;
Mike and Kathy Alexander.

# PROLOGUE

This story starts with Father Lehi and the patriarchal blessing he gave to the children of Laman, his oldest son, quoting from the Book of Mormon:

> Wherefore because of my blessing, the Lord God will not suffer that ye perish; wherefore, he will be merciful unto you and unto your seed forever. (2 Nephi 4:7)

> You will see their seed received a blessing of protection and mercy. Five hundred years later, a worthy group of their Kindred became warriors for God and saved a nation.

Behold, two thousand of the sons of those men whom Ammon brought down out of the land of Nephi—now ye have known that these were descendants of Laman, who was the eldest son of our father, Lehi (Alma 56:3).

This story covers a period of about twenty-five to thirty years and three generations: Ammon, the son of King Mosiah and missionary to the Lamanites; Ablon, servant of King Lamoni and convert to the Gospel; his wife, Azal; their son, Heth; Ammon's daughter, Sariah, who married and had a family (Nathan, Ruth, and Naomi); and other family members, cousins Aaron and Joel.

The four sons of King Mosiah—Ammon, Aaron, Omner, and Himni—became an instrument in God's hand to share the

Gospel with their brethren the Lamanites. They taught thousands of Lamanites and changed the Lamanite nation.

This story, *All Were Wounded, None Were Lost*, tells how their grandsons became stripling warriors and fought with the power of God for their families, religion, and country and saved the Nephite nation.

As I begin the telling of this story, I need to give some brief explanations of the people and places in which this story covers. If the reader is not familiar with the peoples of the Book of Mormon, I will give an outline that will make the characters and their actions more understandable to the reader.

The Book of Mormon follows a family who leaves Jerusalem, about 600 BC, builds a ship, and travels to the American continent under the direction of God.

The family is made up of Lehi, who is a prophet called by God; Sariah, his wife; their six sons (Laman, Lemuel, Sam, Nephi, Jacob, Joseph) and daughters.

After settling in the new land, Laman and Lemuel rebelled. They wanted to become the rulers as the older brothers.

The family divided, and over the next five hundred years become bitter enemies. Those following Laman and Lemuel felt they should rule the people, and they took the name of Lamanites. They inherited the land where the family first landed. It was called the land of Nephi. The Lamanites became a wild and bloodthirsty warlike people and continued the hatred for the group called Nephites. The Nephites followed Nephi and left the land of Nephi to escape the hatred of the Lamanites and traveled through much wilderness and met up with other people from Jerusalem and settled in the area of Zarahemla. The Nephites brought with them a record of their language and God's teachings, which they followed. The Nephites were more righteous people.

For five hundred years, the two peoples engaged in many wars and conflicts, killing many thousands on each side.

Both the Lamanites and the Nephites were ruled by kings. The Lamanite's traditions of hatred toward the Nephites were handed down from king to king and taught to the people, and most Lamanites held to those traditions.

The Nephites were ruled by kings. The last two kings were righteous and blessed the people. The Nephites prospered and were blessed by God. They set up a system of government ran by judges, and they enacted laws to govern a free people. As our story begins, the four sons of the last king refused to become king. Instead, they want to travel to the land of Nephi and become missionaries to a wild and furious Lamanite people to bring souls unto God.

# CHAPTER I

Ammon loaded the last of his belongings in the two-wheeled cart and motioned to his sweetheart, Racheal, that it was time to leave. Racheal hugged her mother-in-law, clinging to her extra long, feeling deep within that this was good-bye forever. Moist eyes came easy as Racheal picked Sariah out of Grandpa Mosiah's arms. Sariah squeaked, reaching for the comfortable hugs she loved so much.

Ammon looked out toward the street leading to the gates of Zarahemla and the road beyond. He knew an epic journey was beginning today.

People pushed handcarts loaded with fruits and vegetables coming from the fields to the lower markets. This bustling city came alive each morning as the day started with the rising of the sun.

Ammon loved the sounds of the cartwheels clunking on the stone streets, dog yapping as donkeys brayed in staccato unison to begin a new-morning symphony of marketplace music. This was Ammon's home. He would miss Zarahemla. It was here as a boy that he ran the streets with his brothers Aaron, Omner, and Himni. In this place, they experienced a conversion to the gospel of Jesus Christ. And it was here he met and married Racheal, the love of his life.

Now he felt the call from the Holy Spirit to lead a group of missionaries to the land of Nephi, to become an instrument in God's hand to preach the gospel to the Lamanites.

Ammon could be king over the land of Zarahemla. He would have none of that. He rejected the invitation, as did Aaron, Omner, and Himni. All desired to give their lives to serve God. Most people in Zarahemla mocked them for this foolhardy quest. But it mattered nothing to the sons of Mosiah.

An angel of God spoke to them. The time to teach the Lamanites the Word weighed heavily on their minds and in their hearts. So the journey began with his wife and child. His brothers and their families, in all sixty-two people, followed Ammon through wilderness over mountains, suffering from the heat and strain of a long, drawn-out trip, praying and fasting for the help of heaven to guide his footsteps and keep them safe.

At last, the party arrived on the borders of the land of Nephi. Here the brothers split up. Each went where they felt inspired by the spirit to travel.

Ammon turned to his left, moved through a pass in some tall craggy mountains, and followed a fast-running stream out into a vast valley below. This was the land of Ishmael, ruled by a king named Lamoni. His father reigned as king over the whole area of Nephi. Lamoni governed under his regime.

As Ammon came into the land, he surveyed the villages strung along the waterway: fields and pasture out toward the mountains, the king's palace at the center of the main town, living quarters on the right side of the house for the king's family, a great meeting hall in the center where the king met with his subjects and held feasts, the guard's garrison occupied the left-wing of the building, and weapons stored on the walls and in rooms ready for use if the need arose.

Gardens surrounded the building on three sides. Much of the food for the king's family grew in these gardens. Along the street, a row of homes stood facing the main road from the king's house. It was smaller but neat and homey and well cared for.

Each servant received a large plot of ground to build a comfortable home and garden to provide for his family while in the employ of the king. The only drawback was if a servant lost the king's flocks while tending them, he was put to death—a custom that carried on for many years.

Ammon secured his family outside the borders, with the plan to get settled and move them in with him soon. Then Ammon walked cautiously, moving through the fields of the king, knowing of the danger.

There he was taken and bound. Two Lamanite guards dragged Ammon before King Lamoni.

"We found the Nephite invading your fields."

Lamoni questioned Ammon, and a bond between the two men began to develop. Lamoni liked Ammon so much he offered one of his daughters as a wife for Ammon.

Ammon spoke kindly. "Thank you. I have a wife and daughter. Though I would like to be your servant and live among your people."

"Okay, you may help care for my flocks with my other servants. I have a home you and your wife may have down the street from here."

*****

Ablon, a descendant of Laman, with thick dark hair, bright shining brown eyes, a clean jawline, and an intelligent forehead always carried himself as a man with a purpose. His wife, Azal, his childhood sweetheart, was raised in the land of Ishmael, a more settled part of the Lamanites nation. They loved each other and nurtured their children, Heth and Hanna. Ablon acquired a position with King Lamoni as a servant to care for his flocks. He was an honest Lamanite who hated any Nephite and believed the Great Spirit governed all things.

His purpose in working for the king was for gain like most young Lamanites. He was not above stealing a little or plundering from others. It was a common practice. If one could keep from being killed by King Lamoni for losing his flocks, you could make yourself some extra loot in a year.

King Lamoni served under his father, the Lamanite king over the whole land of Nephi. Lamoni governed with a stern but gentle hand, but many servants died because of lost flocks. It happened for many years, and the servants knew it was the chance they took working for the king.

The land of Ishmael, which King Lamoni ruled, spread over a vast plain. It was perfect for raising sheep and goats of all kinds. The grass grew tall because of the abundant rain and mild climate.

Surrounded by mountains on the west and north, the villages were protected from hotter sunny days. Magnificent pine trees dotted the landscape. It was a pleasant setting for the inhabitants.

As a servant of the king, he received the task to drive the flocks each day to a place called the waters of Sebus.

Starting forward on a bright sunny morning, he could not believe his eyes, out of the corral came a Nephite. Ablon's blood boiled, seeing this child of a liar. How could this enemy of his people be here serving the king? Something about this man was like no other Ablon ever met.

Ammon was dressed in simple clothes, longish hair past his ears. His bright brown eyes watch every move of his fellow servants. Broad shoulders muscles were bulging under his tunic. A broad forehead and ample nose graced his face. A humble air followed this man, a power that could influence others for good. He always moved with purpose and style. Ammon was a servant of God.

The Lamanite found out quickly that Ammon was hard to hate. This man's personality made you want to be his friend and want to be like him.

As they started forward with the flocks, the two of them soon became friends.

Ablon inquired, "Your name is Ammon? Who are you, and how did you come to serve the king?"

Ammon looked directly into Ablon's eyes and said, "I am here with a message from God for you and your people."

A quiet shiver touched Ablon's mind and heart. He said, "Did you come alone?"

"My three brothers came and several other missionaries. Also, my wife, Rachel, and our daughter, Sariah."

"You came here to serve the king?" Ablon queried.

"Yes," Ammon stated. "I want to share the great joy I have found in my life with you and your king." Ammon asked, "Do you have a wife and children?"

A bright smile of pride burst across Ablon's face. "Yes, I have a beautiful wife. We have known each other all our lives. We grew up together, married when we were young. We have a strong young son,

Heth, and daughter, Hanna. "That's why I am here working for the king to help support my family."

Ammon asked, "Wwhat do you have planned for your children?"'

*This man does care for his fellow servants and the king*, thought Ablon.

At Ammon's side, Ablon saw it for the first time, the Sword of Laban. It was long as a man's arm, full as your hand at the handle, two edges tapering to a sharp point. The hilt was pure gold with jewels mounted at the end of the handle. Forged from the finest steel, shiny brilliant silver, it never dulled with age. One stroke from this blade could remove a man's arm or deal a death blow across the helmet of an enemy. A tattered sheath made of thick leather protected the sword, making it easy to carry, with a wide belt. It was surprisingly light and very balanced. Every person chosen to bear this sword was protected and blessed with inspiration, fighting in the cause of the Lord.

The sword carried a blessing of protection for five hundred years. Nephi felt it. Jacob, King Benjamin, Mosiah, Ammon, Helaman, Mormon, Moroni—all felt the benefit of the sword's miraculous power. How it had retained its brightness was a living witness of the power of God. As it hung at Ammon's side, it looked as though the man that wore it was one of the great kings or prophets of the past.

\*\*\*\*\*

The waters of Sebus sat near the bottom of two massive mountains, one jetting out toward the south, the other pointing southwest, opening to a flat plane to the west. If you drove your flocks between the points and blocked the west escape, they could all go to the water and the herders could control them. There is a lot of thicket growing near the watering ponds, where someone could hide and scatter the animals as they came to drink, which was a common practice for most herders. Stealing a few sheep or goats as the herders brought the animals to water added to a significant loss for the king over a year.

If you kept from getting killed, it was an excellent way to steal and plunder some other flocks.

The day was bright and cloudless, not too hot. You would say it was a comfortable summer morning. Ammon moved among the flocks, gently humming to calm the lambs and goats as they moved toward the points in the far distance. The other servants began to act nervous and shaky as they neared the end of the first hill. The flocks sensed the water and began to rush up the trail past the brush. Things commenced happening in very rapid order. The front of the herd reached the water. They started drinking, and the animals behind slammed into the animals in front, causing a great commotion. At the same time, two giant white dogs came bounding out of the brush on the command of their masters hiding in the bushes. The perfect plan began to unfold for the plundering Lamanites.

They appeared on each side of the herd, rushing in with the big dogs. Jaws snapping, loud howling, and barking caused the flocks to scatter in all directions.

Ablon thought, *We are dead.*

The sheep were being frightened suddenly by the dogs and screaming men waving swords and clubs heading straight toward them. The only opening was the plains to the west.

The servants of the king stared in unbelief. "How could this happen? Surely the king's flocks will be lost, and he shall put us to death."

With the thought settling in Ablon's head, *We have lost the king's herds,* he began to wail and moan, "We are dead men. It's happened before. What can we do?"

The men looked to their right. Ammon was kneeling next to the dogs holding a piece of meat, feeding the dogs, scratching behind their ears, and talking to them in a gentle, firm voice. They were licking his hand and wagging their tails.

The thought came. *He can even make friends with ferocious dogs. Who is this man?* All disbelief was interrupted by Ammon's command.

"Follow me. Let us surround the flocks."

With that, everyone rushed forward, dogs in tow.

"Wow, this Nephite could run."

All were at top speed trying to keep up. The herd consisted of goats, sheep, donkeys, cows, and a few horses—all making a beeline for the plains to the west. Within five minutes, the servants were up with them.

Another five minutes, all the frightened animals were surrounded. The dogs loved their new friend and obeyed his commands.

They suspect their owners so mistreated these hounds. A little food and kindness and their loyalty turned to a new master. Ammon gave instructions to each of the men. Knowing him for a short time, all the servants knew whatever he told them to do, they will do without question.

"Spread out. Move the herd slowly back toward the water. I will take care of these Lamanites."

As Ammon trotted away in front of the flocks, the idea came to the other herders.

*Those poor Lamanites are in for the surprise of their life.*

The sword hung at his side. Reaching into his pouch, he drew a sling and a handful of smooth round stones.

The Lamanites surrounding the water were mainly from two families. They lived in a village five miles away and were known for being mean, ornery, bullies, lazy, and always more willing to plunder than work.

Their leader was a big grungy pillager with long dirty, stringy black hair; small beady eyes; yellow teeth; and large lips with a four-inch-long whitish scar down the side of his right cheek. He was about the same height as Ammon but not nearly as muscular. A large club hung at his side, and a short sword waved above his head in his right hand. He was screaming for all to hear.

"Is this the king's guard, one Nephite and a bunch of chickens. I was hoping for a real fight today before we take these flocks."

Just then, there was a loud thud, and his younger brother standing next to him toppled over with a grunt and lay motionless on the ground. A rapid succession of smooth stones rained down on the first row of Lamanites advancing toward Ammon. Two more ugly thieves paid the price for being within range. Down they went. Each caught a stone between the eyes, never to open them again. Another turned to move sideways away from the line of fire. Taking one in the side of the head, he tripped over a dead body and fell face down in the dust.

The leader was enraged. His men were dropping like flies. He rushed forward, screaming at Ammon, *"I will kill you myself."* Froth dribbled out of his mouth and down his chin.

In one blinding motion, this impressive Nephite jumped to his left and reached for the hilt of his sword. There was a flash of silver light that glistened in the morning sun. The sword waved high above Ammon's head. With the swiftness and speed of a striking snake, it came down, causing almost a whistling sound as it cut through the air and struck its target just above the right shoulder and below the right ear. The Lamanite leader slumped to his knees, and his headless body flopped in a heap on the ground.

The second wave of Lamanites came in a full charge, clubs and swords waving in the air. Ammon moved with fluid motion. The Sword of Laban dealt blow after blow with lighting speed and accuracy. There was no wasted motion, no hesitation. There was flashing light, wailing, and screaming as it detached several arms from would-be warriors. Clubs and swords were falling at every stroke. The sword and its power of protection were manifest. The man of God that wielded this sword received excellent protection.

The fray was over in a short time. Having dispatched the thieves, they turned to water the flocks and herds of King Lamoni.

Ablon stood with his mouth gaping open wide. He didn't know whether to cheer or kneel in reverence to this warrior.

"What just happened?" he shouted. "Who are you?"

Ammon acted as though this was just another day in caring for the animals of the king.

"I am just a man. Let's get these animals back to the pastures."

The guards gathered the arms to take to the king with this fantastic tale.

# CHAPTER 2

## *King Lamoni's Palace*

Ammon's joy was overflowing. He returned King Lamoni's flocks to the grazing pastures. A feeling of being an instrument in Gods' hand was here. He knew a teaching opportunity would present itself. Ammon impressed to continue with the orders he received from the captain of the guard. He caught the horses, two white geldings, full of life, stomping, blowing puffs of air from enlarged nostrils. They were ready for the harnesses and a trip out of the barn. Ammon hooked them to the chariot, then went into the palace to see what the Lord would provide in this teaching moment.

While Ammon was caring for the horses, his fellow servants recounted to the king all that happened to them at the waters of Sebus, how Ammon was unable to be killed or even touched by the Lamanites. They began to say that he was the Great Spirit or some superhuman man because they could not believe that anyone had such power. And to be sure, they testified that he was a friend of the king.

King Lamoni became frightened because of the servants he had put to death as they lost his flocks at Sebus. He started to tremble and sweat. From his earliest childhood, the teaching of a Great Spirit was taught to him by his father. Because he was the king, he assumed everything he did was right, even killing his servants. Now Lamoni was not sure.

He asked his servants, "Where is this man?"

"He is caring for the horses and making ready your chariot."

*This man is more faithful than any servant I have ever had,* he thought.

Wonder and amazement came into Lamoni's heart.

*How could he face such a being? What would he say? Would he be stricken down because of his mistakes because of the traditions of his father's? Would this man do to him as he did to the Lamanites at the waters of Sebus? Was he the Great Spirit that always attended the Nephites?*

As Lamoni ran these thoughts through his mind, it seemed that Ammon was here to help him and his people.

How strange, a pile of arms was lying on the floor in front of him. The fact that this man could subdue an army by himself, and yet he was a servant doing his duty better than anyone ever served. Lamoni let out a long slow breath as Ammon entered the room, the Spirit whispered the thoughts of Lamoni's mind to Ammon. The teaching moment Ammon had desired was going very well. He knew if the king and his household would accept God and repent, many of his people would also.

He was about to turn and leave when the chief captain said, "Oh, Great One, the king desires you to stay."

Ammon turned and spoke to the king. "What do you want me to do?"

But there was no answer.

Ammon stood silent, waiting for the king to answer.

A long silence continued.

Finally, Ammon asked again, "What do you want me to do?" Now Ammon knew what King Lamoni wanted of him. He spoke. "Is it because I protected your herds and servants at the waters of Sebus and with the sword cut off the arms of the attackers?"

The king was amazed. Ammon could read his thoughts, and that scared him. King Lamoni summoned his courage and asked, "Who are you? Are you the Great Spirit that knows everything?"

"No, I am just a man, like you. But I do have a portion of his spirit with me. Oh, mighty King, will you listen and follow what I will tell you about this Great Spirit and his power and teachings?"

"Yes, tell me more."

Ammon smiled and began to teach the household of King Lamoni.

Ablon settled on a wooden bench within hearing range of this man of God and began to open his mind to all Ammon taught. A warm feeling washed over him. He knew in his heart what Ammon was teaching was true. He was an eyewitness to the power Ammon possessed and the Sword that protected him.

"I will share this with my family as soon as I get home. I will tell them of this Jesus Christ and his great love for us."

Suddenly King Lamoni slumped over in his chair and fell on the floor.

"What was happening?" Ablon stepped forward. "I must help the king." He reached down and held him in his arms. The other servants gathered around, and they slowly picked Lamoni up and carried him to his bed.

Lying him down, Ablon sank to the floor as many of the other servants did. In his mind, a bright light appeared and the words of Ammon speaking of one Jesus Christ came softly over the waves of music and the feeling of immense love from a being who knew every thought and intent of his heart. His only desire was to share this feeling and knowledge with his family and friends. When he recovered, his life changed forever.

Ablon experienced a vision of angels. He then forsook all of his past sins and was redeemed by God.

Ablon went home after his time with the king, wanting to share this experience with Azal, his wife; Heth, his son; and little Hannah. He loved his children. This new faith would bless and protect his family. It was what Ammon had and what he wanted. He became one of the first teachers to his fellow servants and a companion to Ammon as they taught the people of King Lamoni.

Ablon began reading the scriptures Ammon brought with him. Azal wanted to know more also. The two families spent several days together talking about the commandments, sharing meals, and sacred teaching time. Heth and Sariah tried to ignore each other at first. Soon they became friends. competing in everything the families did.

Heth thought he was always stronger and faster.

19

One night after a family get-togather with the two families, Ablon spoke up.

"The big celebration is coming after planting season. And I hear there is a race for young people with the prize to the winner, the Golden Jacket."

Heth's eyes opened fully. The legend of the Golden Jacket is known over the whole land of Ishmael. Young people would come from every corner of King Lomani's empire to compete for the golden coat. The person who won the jacket became the champion of the villages. Everyone respected and revered the winner of the Golden Jacket.

The past winners of this prize coat became leaders in the villages and chiefs among the local people. Great respect was given to them at gathering and celebrations. Each would have an honored place to sit among the leaders of the kingdom. They are always known as the remarkable ones for winning this race.

The jacket was woven by an old Lamanite woman with help from her two daughters. This would be year number twenty for creating the jacket. She used the most delicate wool dyed bright golden yellow. She fashioned it after a long coat with sleeves and wide lapels, a high collar, and golden buttons on each lapel. There is a great sunburst on the back, showing a blazing sun shining over the mountains and kingdom below. All are done in reds and yellows with a blue sky and green trees and fields.

Never in the history of this race had a woman won. Several years ago King Lomani agreed that all who wanted could race. The only rule was the participants must be under the age of seventeen.

It became a race of endurance, stamina, and skill. Many Lamanites used this race as a measurement for becoming a warrior and a man.

The race consisted of three parts: strength, skill, and speed. First, everyone carried a ten-pound rock in a sack over their shoulder, going uphill for one mile. Next, with a spear in hand, each contestant had to run at a straw dummy. They have to stab the dummy, roll over, stand up, and run to the next five hundred yards apart, repeating the same stabbing move until they went through five models. Then they would throw the spear into a target, getting points for how close to the center the spear stuck. Then they would pick up a bow and shoot three out of five arrows in a mark next to the spear. This part of the race covered two and one half miles, up a steep mountain. Down a winding trail off the mountain around a lake and back toward the starting line.

*****

Sariah told Heth, "I am going to win the jacket."

Heth laughed out loud. "Ba-ha, you? You're too skinny and weak. It's mine for the taking. Just stay out of my way when I get going. I'll leave you in the dust."

Sariah just smiled. "We shall see."

Together the pair practiced each day running, throwing spears, shooting, carrying rocks. It was grueling practice. Heth would always be one step ahead of Sariah at the finish.

The enviable taunting came. "How's second place look?" or "Can you keep up today?"

All the while, Sariah held back. She was fast. Natural speed came from long slender legs and a long stride. While Heth's more husky body and legs pumped up and down many hundred times, Sariah glided along effortlessly, able to increase her speed at anyplace along the course. The spear gave her no problems. Nine times out of ten, she hit the center of the target. The bow and arrows flew straight and true for Sariah. The rock was like carrying a bucket of water, which she did several times a day for her mother.

The day of the celebration came.

Sariah called her father over to the side before the race began.

"Dad," she said, "I can beat Heth today. I know I can. We have practiced together. I've watched him when he gets tired I can take him on the hills, but should I beat him? Will it embarrass him too much?"

Ammon looked at his daughter. His heart felt joy. She was such a sweet spirit, much like her mother.

"My dear," he said, "do what you feel is right."

"He has teased me every day we practiced, and I let him win. Setting the poor boy up to think he was just a little faster, which today he shall see he is not, Dad. I think I will teach him a lesson that the race does not always go to the strongest or the fastest, but it goes to the smartest. Today I will run a smart race and win the Golden Jacket."

"That's a good idea, Sariah. But don't rub it in too much."

*****

A judge called all the participants to the starting line. Each carried a bag with a rock in it. There were all sizes of kids, each with hopes of winning the Golden Jacket displayed near the finish line.

Sariah was only worried about two kids. A tall lad from the village over near the forest with long legs and small eyes that darted around, trying to see everything at once. No one practiced as hard as Heth. Sariah was sure she practiced harder.

Now was showtime.

*Smack!*

Off they went, bunched together like a herd of sheep heading for the water. Heth broke from the pack, sprinted up the hill, legs pumping and arms swinging. As the gang hit the hill, the rock became heavy and most slowed to a brisk walk. Sariah shouldered the stone high on her back, moved away from the crowd, and found the hill suddenly steeper than she remembered.

Her sandals slipped a little in the dirt. But she regained her balance, shifted the rock, and found more speed. Up the hill she went, like so many days before chasing Heth. Sariah could see his legs pumping up and down. His rock was slipping down by his knees, which slowed him down. She passed him just before they reached the summit of the hill and dropped the stone in a marked circle.

Quickly, Sariah grabbed a spear, charged headlong into the first figure, and rolled over. She jumped up and sprinted toward number two, five hundred yards away, with Heth right on her heels. The tall kid was a distant third. Practicing every day proved to pay off now.

She kicked it into another gear, breathing very lightly as she rammed the spear, rolled, and was off again in a flash.

Heth was up with her. His breathing was heavy and labored. Beads of sweat streamed down his face. Panting like a dog on a hot day, he shouted, "Getting tired yet," to Sariah.

"No, I am waiting for the killer hill."

They finished the second stage at the same time. Heth's spear hit one inch from the center of the target. Sariah's hit the center.

She grabbed the bow, and her first arrow missed the target. "Sariah," she said to herself, "slow down. This is your best event." She brought another arrow up and slowly released. *Twang*. Dead center. Again, *twang*. Dead center. One more was all she needed, and she could be off. Sariah took a deep breath just as Heth fired his last arrow dead center, and he was off and running.

*Twang*. The arrow flew straight and true and hit the center. She dropped the bow and looked up to see Heth sprinting away.

As he looked back, Sariah went past him.

As the long sloping hill came into view, it seemed ten miles long. Heth's legs ached. He pushed too hard in the spear-throwing; now he was lagging. How could she be so good at everything? Look at her, skipping along, her feet barely touching the ground, striding as if she could run forever. What could he do? Push. He must work harder. She was not going to beat him.

Every day they practiced he had outran her. Or did he? She never tried to pass him. She ran right behind him. If he sped up, she would speed up. If he slowed down, she would slow down. Sariah used him to train herself, to beat him. Now he could see how stupid he was. She knew when he got tired and how much to push herself to stay ahead of Heth. She was working it to perfection.

Halfway up the killer hill, her legs began to ache and her lungs were burning. Sariah slowed her pace. She was fifty yards ahead of anyone. Heth and the tall skinny kid were in a battle for second. The gang was laboring, coming up the hill.

Her mind wandered, *Should I let Heth win?* Again, the feeling came. *No, push on*. And with that thought, Sariah topped the summit of the killer hill, finding new inner strength. She bolted off like a burst of wind around the pond and back, past the cheering crowd. Slowing to look behind, she saw Heth and the skinny kid neck and neck, working past the lake, coming in a great cloud of dust. Sariah crossed the finish line and settled on a grassy spot next to her father.

"Great race, honey. You are the best runner in all of the country today. I am so proud of you. You deserve the jacket."

Heth came in second by a head length. He collapsed in the dirt and finally came around. Looking up, he saw a beautiful girl holding a water bag, saying, "How is second place? Would you like a drink?"

A few moments later, the judge raised his hands to quite the rumbling noise of the crowd. "We have a new champion." Helped Sariah stand up on a large block of wood, the judge presented her with the Golden Jacket. She slipped it on, smiled, waved to everyone, and jumped down. She turned to Heth and said, "If you're nice to me, I'll let you wear it some time."

Heth rolled his eyes, beaten by this girl, but he knew right then he loved her.

*****

A significant change came to Ablon's family.

Heth was excited at first by this new religion. Later, he started to resent the restrictions of keeping the commandments. It seemed they were forced upon him. Heth enjoyed the feelings of love when with his family or Sariah's family. When with his friends, he wanted to be part of the gang.

Heth wanted to be a warrior to steal and plunder, kill Nephites, and follow his so-called friends. How could he believe in a God he could not see? Why couldn't he take from those who were weak? He was a bold Lamanite. In his mind, a battle raged. Feelings he never experienced before caused Heth to get angry over such little things. His temper seemed uncontrollable.

Heth was proud and strong. When the jawing and name-calling started, that's what pushed him to the point. He broke.

One night, the conversation turned to the competition. The girl won, the first time in the history of the celebration. The insults began.

Heth could take it no longer, and he started throwing punches at everyone and everybody. He kicked, clawed, screamed, and made a total fool of himself. Heth, being an excellent and fierce fighter, no one in the crowd was willing to face this wild man. They just laughed, taunted him about being beaten by a girl, and being a servant to the Nephites. Most kept out of arm's length, or they felt his rage as Heth cleared the court in the center of the town.

Then he stumbled and fell on his face, swearing he was through with this new religion his family forced upon him.

Heth had one weak spot in his resolve to rebel, Sariah.

Heth withdrew from his family, became sullen and aloof with his parents, spent most of the time with his new friends. Sariah always seemed close. He saw her at the market, on the roadside, or in the village center. They were friends. He did admit the happiest days he spent was the long walks with Sariah, sitting by the water's edge, talking of the future, each growing more in love as they spent time together.

Sariah kept saying, "We are only friends. We are too young. I want to marry someone of my faith." And closer and closer, she slipped into the feeling of deep love for this young man. Even with all his faults, she knew he was one of the finest young men she knew. And he was handsome. The great dilemma was coming, and she knew it.

What would she do? Where did her heart lie, with Heth or with God? That was her decision to make. After several hours of prayer, pondering, and fasting, she finally knew the answer.

# CHAPTER 3

## *Lost but Not Forever*

Sariah sat at the edge of the stream, dangling her feet in the freshwater. Her mind drifting over the last few days. She liked this young man, but did she love him?

Heth was hoping that he had said the right thing. You must be careful when trying to impress this girl. You can't be too aloof or too harsh, and don't say something stupid. It is a complicated maneuver while trying to look so charming. Heth stood torn between his feelings for this slender brown-eyed beauty and his dislike for this new way of life being forced on him by his parent, although exciting at first. But now, three years later, they were outcast. The change had been remarkable. Heth enjoyed the time spent with Ammon and his family.

Sariah, was kind, funny, gorgeous, and always happy. She was tough also and could run as fast as any boy…and smart. There was a time when he tried to ignore her, but it was useless. She won his heart the day she won the race and the Golden Jacket. That had him upset. Heth wanted it both ways—he wanted to marry Sariah; he also wanted to be in the gang, to live like a real Lamanite. It was a sign of weakness to have a woman control your every thought. And he decided, in his young adolescent brain, that he would demand that if she loved him, she would forget this God of her father's and became a true Lamanite wife. Now how to present this idea to Sariah?

The leaders in the gang he hung around were always pushing their hatred toward the Nephites, explaining how it was justified because of five hundred years of tradition. To be mean and cruel to all weaker people and to prosper by killing, stealing, plundering was a natural way of life. Heth wanted to feel this way, but when he was with Sariah, he could not think of these things. The battle in his head went back and forth. His thought process became warped, and he convinced himself it was just a matter of being persuasive rather than weak.

So the showdown with Sariah was coming. He knew he could win her heart and convince her to marry him and be an obedient wife. Little did he realize just how smart this young lady was, but he was soon to find out.

They slipped off to a quiet place, peaceful and secluded.

Sariah and Heth spent several hours here talking, of God and his son Jesus Christ, families, children, and life together, feelings of the Spirit, and the excitement of young love.

Sariah took a long breath, let it out slowly, and began, "Heth, you can't have it both ways. You have a choice to make. I know what we have is the Gospel of God. I will not change my mind, and I think you know the same thing. You somehow think that you can have a foot in each camp. But you know what Joshua said, 'Choose yea this day.' Well, I'm telling you the same thing. Choose your path with a good future or back with your so-called friends. But I will not follow where you're heading."

The words hit him like a punch in the gut. He had gone over this in his mind.

"How can you say that? I thought you loved me? What has changed, Sariah?" he shouted, a little too loud.

"You have," she shot back, a little louder.

Heth, knew he had lost. How could he present his case? Sariah knew him too well. He had lost this argument and, with it, any hope of changing her mind.

Sariah sat with her feet in the water, looking so young and beautiful.

He had lost her, or so Heth thought. He turned to leave with a puff of forced air out his nostrils.

Sariah looked away as her eyes filled with tears. "Good-bye, Heth," she said in a soft, low voice.

Heth turned to trot away and then broke into a full run, not wanting to burst into tears. His heart was broken and was hurting so much he could hardly breathe. His mind raced. *I will show her. Someday she would regret her discussion, but it would be too late.* He felt the stinging blow of true love, and it hurt.

Heth pouted for several days. Stupidity settling in his young mind for revenge. He went to see his new friends. They were drinking stout wine, laughing, cussing, and swearing. They were going to kill some people and rid this land of this new religion.

"We shall see if their God will protect them now."

Drunk and stirred up by these white Lamanites, the mob began to grow in numbers. There was a hatred for the people of Ammon. Jealously and deep-seated revenge drove the crowd into a frenzy. The army grew each day until there were three thousand bloodthirsty warriors intent on killing the people of Ammon.

Heth joined in with them but never feeling engaged in the prospect of killing people, especially those he loved. How could he do this? He was beginning to see that following the crowd was a hard way to live.

# CHAPTER 4

## *The People of God*

Heth was a little dizzy. His head ached, and his stomach felt like it would empty at any moment. He had eaten nothing this whole day, only drinking. He sat on a makeshift seat near the front of the mob. A tall, skinny man was jumping and screaming in such a fashion. It was comical, but Heth did not feel like laughing.

This man, whose name was Akish, the leader of the mob, hated the people of God. He was an evil and dark man that would slit your throat if you had something he could steal from you. His eyes were sunken in his oversized head, red and bloodshot, sagging on each side of a large hooked nose. He spit every time he spoke. Everyone tried to stay back and out of range.

Heth had an uneasy feeling being around him. How could he follow the wretched foul man? His mind went back to Sariah. Why had he ended it so soon with her? What a fool, but the battle inside his head continued. Heth remembered the story his grandfather would tell him.

"Son, in your mind, there is a battle between a White Wolf and Black Wolf every day."

"Which wolf wins?" Heth asked.

His grandfather would grin a sly smile and say, "It depends on which one you feed."

For a long time, Heth could not understand what that meant. Today, he knew. It was a battle between good and evil choices, your thoughts and actions. Today he was feeding the Black Wolf. It was a dark feeling that caused him to feel sad and foreboding. Anger welled up in his heart, and he was looking for a fight. Everything irritated him.

The leader, Akish, screamed, "Let's kill some Nephites."

Chanting, they rushed out into the street.

The people of God were coming out of the synagogue—Heth's family, Sariah, Rachel, her mother, and many children, men, and women. They saw the army coming with clubs and swords. There was no fear in their eyes as they knelt before the oncoming soldiers.

The blood began. No fighting or crying, just praising God and willing to keep the covenant each person made. They would not take up arms any more in this life. All would rather die by the sword than break this covenant.

Ammon stood inside the synagogue teaching. He suffered a profound personal loss that day. Several years before, his wife, Rachel, came from Zarahemla with him. A daughter was born to them. Both agreed the name Sariah would serve her well. No other children came to them. Rachel was often very ill and spent much time in bed. Ammon cared for her nonstop when he was home. As the years passed, Sariah became the housekeeper. Rachel was frail, but her resolve was firm and gentle. All the people loved her because of her kindness. Her only desire was to serve others.

The day the army of the Lamanites came to kill the people of God, Rachel stood before them with hands raised high. In a powerful firm voice, she pleaded with those young men to turn back and listen to their hearts and don't make war on the people of God.

Akish raised a club, and Rachel fell silent to the ground.

Heth stood with a sword just a few feet away, witnessing what just happened. His temper flashed. He would kill Akish. Why were these white Lamanites so evil? Heth was more muscular and taller than Akish. He loathed this snake. A flash of anger raced through Heth's mind. He stood and spun around in a blink of a second. He watched this pure, sweet woman crumple and close her eyes. The sword waved high above his head, ready for one swift death blow to end the life of the evil man. In his mind, a voice spoke. A still, small voice yet clear and calm.

"Heth, what good will it do you to kill this man? Rachel is here with me. You need to help take care of Sariah and raise a family. Everything will work out fine. She loves you, and you know you love her."

There was silence.

Heth broke inside. His gut wretched, and his eyes locked on Sariah. She was kneeling next to her mother, sobbing.

Ammon rushed from the building and knelt bent over his companion and pleaded, "Please, God, let her live."

The last words Rachel spoke were, "Ammon, my dear Ammon."

Heth dropped his sword and stepped between the oncoming Lamanites and the children. Heth knew what he wanted in life— Sariah, to live with her, as husband and wife, or to die with her praising God. His days of rebellion was over. A lifetime commitment burned within him, to never question his feelings for Sariah and his family. Heth wanted to live and worship God and raise a family in peace.

However, it looked like he would most likely die before he could make things right with Sariah or repent of the foolish decisions he had made in the past month.

As always, God works miracles every day. Heth witnessed a miracle before his eyes. The mob stopped. Many young Lamanites of the army were dropping their weapons and kneeling with the people of God, making the same choice Heth made—to never take up arms to kill or fight again. He rushed to Sariah's side and looked into those deep brown eyes and begged her forgiveness. With tears streaming down both of their faces, they knelt and gave thanks to God for all the miracles of that day.

Ammon slowly lifted the limp body of his sweetheart in his arms. He bowed his head and made his way down the street to his home to find a final resting place for Racheal. How could he go on?

Sariah and Heth meet Ammon at the house.

Friends came to give support and comfort.

Her grave was on a hill overlooking the valley next to their small home.

Ammon mourned the loss of Racheal.

One night sitting, reading his scriptures, this part of a verse came to rest in his mind.

"I have loved thee with an everlasting love," the Spirit whispered. "She is yours forever, my son. You will come to me when your time on earth is completed."

*****

Heth and Sariah married soon after the death of Sariah's mother, having a small wedding with friends and family.

The tradition in the land of Ishamial for several years followed Lamanite custom: a newly married couple lived with the groom's parents. Heth and Sariah moved into the upper rooms of the home of Ablon and Azal. It became a comfortable arrangement for everyone. Ammon lived in a small dwelling just through the fields and became a frequent visitor to their home.

Life was pleasant at first for the new couple. Heth worked in the fields, growing crops, and built houses and all sorts of buildings. His talent as a master builder kept him busy all seasons of the year. He was known as honest and hardworking, which caused some jealousy and hatred among the Lamanites. For the most part, Heth ignored the negative comments and the loathsome enemies that liked to cause fights or instigate trouble for anything good or decent. Life with Sariah was happy and exciting.

They soon found themselves parents of a strong baby boy. What to name him? Heth thought maybe Ammon after his grandfather. Sariah thought Seth. Then one day, shortly after his birth, his parents looked in the scriptures. Nathan, the prophet grabbed their attention. So it was. Their firstborn son was named Nathan. He looked much like his grandfather Ammon, and that pleased Ammon.

Together they would sit on the back porch as the sun settled on the landscape. Ammon would hum tunes to Nathan and tell him stories of King Benjamin, Nephi, Sam, Enos, and Grandfather Mosiah. Nathan would lay and coo and giggle, and Ammon would smile and say, "Rachael loved babies." Then they would both nod off to sleep for a while.

A daughter came to Heth and Sariah next, Namoi. Her name also came from the scriptures.

*****

One day, when Namoi was just starting to walk, about one year old, and Nathan was three, Sariah gathered the kids. She needed to go to the market in the central village with a list of purchases. It was not long but necessary. She wanted some salt and other spices, some cloth, and some leather. She also needed flour and seeds for a melon Heth loved. She grew them but forgot to save any seeds from the last harvest. Sariah knew a merchant who sold all kinds of seeds in the market place. She would inquire of him to find the melon seed. His stall was over on the far side of the village, so that is where she would start.

Sariah hitched up the donkeys to the two-wheeled cart. She loaded the kids in, and off they went to the market. It was a windy day, cloudy, and overcast. Namoi cried most of the way, and Nathan wanted to, "Dri da crat like Dad."

Sariah thought about turning around and going home. Then she said to herself, "I've come this far. I'll just go on."

The market was crowded, with groups of soldiers pushing and shoving everyone out of their way. The company they belonged to was preparing to march to a distant city, and they were buying food and supplies.

Sariah skirted the central market place and stopped at the seed merchant, with Namoi still screaming and Nathan running off, disappearing as soon as his feet hit the ground.

She yelled, "Nathan, come back here right now."

He poked his head from under a blanket hanging over a pole and smiled at her. "Here I am."

"Stay close by me, please." She scowled.

She found her seeds and some others. She paid for them and turned to leave. "No, Nathan!"

As they were entering the market, two shifty-looking Lamanites saw this young mother with two little kids and followed them inside the store. The lady had to hold the young baby in one arm, who was screaming her head off, paying for here purchases while trying to corral an ambitious three-year-old. It was the perfect time to grab the kid and make a getaway. They could sell him as a slave to any number of lowlife and make a handsome profit. They darted in, grabbed the kid, and were gone out the back door with a hand cupped over his mouth and an iron grip to keep the little guy from squirming out from the captor's arms.

About an hour earlier, Heth, who was working on a building not more than a half-mile from the seed merchant's booth. He received a distinct impression to get down off the scaffolding on which he was working and walk toward the seed merchant's place of business.

He thought, *This seems odd.* But he knew when the impressions came to obey the Spirit.

As he appeared around the corner of the building, he came face-to-face with two surprised Lamanites holding his son in an iron grip with their hands over his mouth. Heth reached out and retrieved his son and set him down out of the way. He grabbed the two misfits by the nape of the neck, slammed their heads together, and let them slump to the ground bleeding and moaning. Then he went to find Sariah and Namoi.

Sariah came sprinting out of the store, tears streaming down her cheeks, screaming, "Nathan, Nathan." Then she collapsed in the arms of the men in her family. They all sat down and thanked God and wept and hugged and wept. Then they got up and finished shopping together and went home.

*****

Life became more difficult each year for the people of God. Heth and Sariah became accustomed to being persecuted, mostly by words and taunting phrases. For the most part, all was forgiven.

The next spring at planting season, Azal and Namoi became deathly sick one day after drinking water drawn from the well by the backyard. Heth climbed down into the well and found someone poisoned it with two dead goats thrown in the well in the night. Heth cleaned them out and spent the day bailing all the water out of the well, then told the family, "We can't use the well for two weeks until clean water runs in."

So now someone would take the donkey cart with water jugs and travel to a spring five miles away, get a load of water, and travel home while the others watched the children.

Ruth, the youngest daughter, was just six months old. Sariah spent most of her time caring for her new baby.

Heth built high fences around the gardens to keep trespassers out. Several times rows of vegetables lay pulled up or smashed by someone stomping through the garden.

Heth went to the village officer with a complaint. He was a large man, lazy and unmotivated to settle quarrels between neighbors, as he saw it. Heth tried to explain it was more than disagreements; it was the destruction of property. His mother-in-law and his little girl almost died from poison well water from dead goats in his well and his garden destroyed several times. Heth was upset.

The officer scratched his belly and said, "I couldn't do anything. I don't have names, and it would be your word against theirs. Doesn't your Nephite religion teach about forgiveness? Maybe you should just forgive them. Ha-ha." He laughed. Then he said, "Go home and ask your God to help you grow a new garden."

It was much the same as all the people of Ammon. They could take this persecution no longer. Coming to gather, they asked, "How can we stop the evil against us?"

Ammon and his brethren counseled with King Anti-Nephi-Lehi and King Lamoni. Word came to them. The Nephites gave the people of Ammon the land of Jershon, which bordered the east sea and the land Bountiful.

It was decided the people of Ammon would move. Heth and Sariah begin to pack their belongings to move to a new home in the land of Jershon.

\*\*\*\*\*

It takes time to organize a company of people to move their whole lives to a new beginning. It was a monumental task for the people of Ammon. Each of the brothers of Ammon—Aaron, Omner, and Himni—would lead a group.

Now each brother spent fourteen years in the service of God teaching and ministering to the Lamanites.

The sons of Mosiah's families had expanded while in this land, and each brother had children and grandchildren moving back to the area of Jershon with them. Three of these grandsons were of the same age: Nathan, Aaron, Joel.

Nathan was Ammon's grandson. Aaron was Aaron's grandson. Joel was Omner's grandson.

Aaron was named after his grandfather on his father's side. His mother is Heth's sister, Hanna. Nathan and Aaron are first cousins. Joel is Omner's grandson.

And that is how the three cousins grow up together in the land of Jershon.

# CHAPTER 5

## *Traveling to a New Home*

The trip toward the land of Zarahemla was long and tedious. The slow-moving company wound out through the flat area of Ishmael, climbing up into the wooded hills where the trails were narrow and often disappeared in the rocks and shale. Ammon, led the way. Ablon and Azal were in this first company. Heth and Sariah with their three children—Nathan, Naomi, and little Ruth—were riding in a cart, as well as everything they owned: a small flock of sheep and goats, chickens, two horses, and two donkeys, and a milk cow. The horses pulled a four-wheel cart with the family in, and the donkeys pulled a smaller cart with the tools and seed. Ablon and Azal walked as did Heth and Sariah.

Heth and Sariah lagged behind his father and mother. The day was extra hot, and the humidity made it feel like walking through a warm water-soaked sponge. Heth's legs ached, and dust gathered on his face and arms. He was moving his young family from their comfortable home to an unknown land, but he knew not to complain.

His mind floated back to the home they recently left. It was built sturdy and functional with open windows to let the breeze move the air around the house. Trees in the courtyard offered shade over the kitchen and eating room. Clean, freshwater just outside the back door was always available for a refreshing drink. The bedrooms upstairs were airy in the hot season and warm and tight when the colder weather came. It was the home of his birth that he shared with his parents, wife, and three children. This was his place of comfort and discovery. His family was so happy now. A new light shone in their eyes. When they made the covenant, everything changed. Heth was a youth at the time. He rebelled at first until he made a choice. It was either Sariah and his family or the gang of Laminates. Heth gazed over at Sariah. It was love when she won the race several years earlier. She fell deeply in love.

They did not know how many people were in the company. Aaron and his family lead a large group, as did Omner and Himni. Lamoni's brother, Anti-Nephi-Lehi, also had a company of people. The train moved slowly up the hills, making a reasonable distance every day. The weather was warm in the mornings and hot in the afternoons. Clouds of dust rose into great bellowing puffs. No rain came most of the journey.

Nathan loved being with his cousins Aaron and Joel, being all the same age. They were with each other most of the time. Nathan considered himself the leader of the three, although Aaron and Joel never followed anything Nathan said. Joel was quiet, never said much, just smiled, and went along with whatever the other two did. Aaron was a worker when chores need doing. It was Aaron first to say, "We will do it." The young boys were always looking for something exciting to take their minds off the long boring trip. Every morning was the same thing—herd the sheep and goats to water and let them graze until it was time to move out. Then as they rode along, it was time to study. Sariah taught her children to read and write from a copy of the ancient record. She instructed them to memorize scriptures, songs, and poems. Music was also part of their education. Her children were good students. Heth and Sariah were very proud of their children. And were the center of their lives.

One day the three boys had more excitement than they could handle. It all started as a typical morning—feeding the animals, eating a quick breakfast, then packing everything up. They began moving out. The company entered a dense forest where the trail almost disappeared alongside a swift stream as it migrated down the slow sloping hills to an unseen lake somewhere below. The young men begged their parents to let them go fishing in the stream as it moved and wound out of the mountains to the left and bubbling over the rocks and dead fallen trees near the trail.

Fresh fish would be an excellent choice for supper, so reluctantly, the parents said, "Yes."

Off they went. Their type of fishing was quite ingenious. The boys made a net out of cloth and thread attached to smooth round rocks along the bottom of the net. It worked very effectively. The three boys were working together. First is finding a slow-moving part of the stream, a pool worked best, where two boys would spread the net in the flow. Then the third boy would make his way upstream; slip into the water with a long stick; and begin moving slowly downstream, poking the stick under the banks and rocks where fish would hide.

This action in the water sent the fish swimming downstream, trying to escape the stick that was disturbing their peace with a good share of the fish moving right into the net. As the fish entered the net, the two boys would pull the ends together and catch eight or ten fish.

Dragging the net to the bank, all three boys scrambled to string the fish on a forked stick, then it was off to the next pool. When they caught enough fish for their families, they wrapped them in the net and lay in the sun to warm up and dry off. Everything went as planned. The fishing was excellent that day.

The boys fish for all their families for supper. They lay out on a grassy hill, soaking in the bright sunshine, and soon fell asleep. The sun was almost setting when the boys stirred. They sat up quickly, rubbed the sleep from their eyes, and looked at each other and the fish, which were dried and stinking already, and the idea of being lost settled in their minds.

"Where are we?" Aaron said, looking up over the hill. How could they have slept so long?

Traveling was so exhausting. Each boy felt rested and ready to find the camp. The only problem was which way was it? Fear gripped their hearts.

A low growing sound came from the top of the hill.

Looking up, an enormous brown rust-colored bear appeared. It rose on its back legs and sniffed the air. The smell of stinking fish started the huge bear lopping downhill toward the boys.

Joel and Aaron screamed at the same time, "Bear! Run!"

Nathan gasped for air, reached down, grabbed the forked stick with the fish on it, and headed downhill right behind Aaron and Joel. In two quick leaps, the bear was on him. Then a still small voice in Nathans's head said, "Drop the fish." With that, Nathan threw the fish out to the right and went past Aaron and Joel, going full speed downhill toward a large tree that grew at the edge of the meadow.

As the boys reached the tree, each jumped and caught a low-hanging branch. Then they scurried up into the higher branches, not knowing that the bear, satisfied for the moment, forgot all about the boys in the tree and was feasting on the stinking fish meant for their family.

They were shaking uncontrollably with the possibility of being lost forever and wild Lamanites lurking in the shadows as the sunset in the west. Three young boys gathered on a big branch.

Nathan said, "We need to say a prayer and ask God's help in keeping us alive until morning."

Never had they prayed so sincere or pleaded so earnestly for help. It would be a lesson that in years to come would be comforting and helpful.

Just as their prayers ended, a loud voice came into earshot. It was Heth, Nathan's father. Nothing sounded as good as his dad's voice and to see several men walking up to the tree.

They were safe and back with their families. Although they lost the fishnet, they learned a great lesson that day.

Back at camp, Nathan hugged his mother. "Mom, your teachings are correct. God answers prayer, and he protects us."

# CHAPTER 6

## *Beginning a New Life*

The new village was a beautiful place for Nathan to live near cousins Aaron and Joel, who lived just over the next hill through the green fields by the big trees that were fun to climb. Jershon was a fun place to explore for three young boys. The fishing was superb in the streams. Nathan's father took him many times camping near the seashore. Although he and Aaron and Joel did not journey off too far by themselves since the bear incident.

Life settled into a comfortable routine work, school, play, and time spent with Dad off in the forest or near the sea. He felt so grown-up when his father would ask him, "Nathan, do you think we should help the new family build a house or go fishing?"

Nathan wanted to say, "Let them build their own house. Let's fish." But he knew what was right. His mother instructed him several times, "Your great-grandfather taught this lesson—'When you are in the service of others, you are in the service of God.'"

Nathan felt deep in his heart how right that was even at twelve years old.

So off they would go to help yet another family settle into the new village, and he never really did mind helping as long as he was with his father. Because after each project, they would slip off for a couple of days and sleep out under the stars and fish, hunt, and sit by the campfire.

Nathan would lie next to his dad and listen to the tales of Heth's boyhood. The story Nathan loved the most was when Heth told of the day he first knew he loved Nathan's mother. He would say, "Your mom was the fastest girl I ever knew, and one day we had a celebration." Nathan never tired of hearing this tale of his parents when they were young and fell in love. Heth would continue, "She beat me hands down that day. Oh, we practiced together every day, and she let me win every day until race day. Then Sariah blew past me like a rabbit trying to escape a fox. Me, being such a stupid male, could not see it until the race was over. And she won the Golden Jacket! The thing that made me first love was, all she said to me after the race was, 'If you are kind to me, I'll let you wear it.' She never mentioned it much after that and put the jacket away to give to someone else in her life sometime in the future. Have you seen it, Nathan?"

"No, Dad. Mom always says, 'I'll show it to you someday when the time is right.'"

"Then I had a rough time in my life, so I rebelled against God and my family. Sariah saved my soul. I am grateful every day for the covenant I made with God never to raise a sword to fight again. The saddest was how Grandmother Rachel died standing for what was right."

It brought tears to Nathan's eyes each time anyone repeated it. He loved his father and wanted to be like him in every way.

*****

This morning the problems of life seemed heavy because Nathan wanted to spend the day with Aaron and Joel. Still, he had chores to do first, milk the cow. Nathan stared blankly into space. What had happened? That miserable cow was missing again. She had pushed her way through the pickets in the fence and was nowhere in sight. He silently hoped she would fall in a hole and die. But then she would stink and be a mess to clean up. Nathan pretty much knew where the old bag of bones was—over in the pass between the village and the main road leading on out to Zarahemla, eating weeds. Her milk would be rank the next few days. He sauntered out through the fields and crossed over the stream.

His father decided on this place when they first came to Jershon. It was the perfect place to establish a new life. The soil was fertile, plenty of water, the weather mild, and great neighbors.

Grandpa Ammon lived just down the road. It was a great life. Heth was a very kind man. He believed in working hard when it was time to work and playing hard when it was time to play.

Heth became more like Christ each year, a great father to his children, a wonderful husband, friend to all. He loved his family very much. Because of Heth's fear over came as skill as a builder, he and Nathan worked on almost every home in the village, as more and more Lamanites came to settle with the people of Ammon.

Nathan's mother taught each day. The three children spent time studying from the scriptures, working hard, and learning respect. Sariah demanded obedience to family rules. It was a safe and happy way to live.

Except for this morning. Nathan was annoyed with this head-strong cow. He would find her and bring her back, then fix the hole in the fence, and things would be fine. He broke into a quick trot through the fields and down the road to find the cow. Rounding the bend, Nathan slowed to a walk. Looking up, he saw his grandfather driving the cow down the road toward him. Ammon was still a king-ly-looking man. His once dark hair was white. It gave him a stately and confident presence. For just an instant, Nathan saw in his mind's eye a younger Ammon, with the Sword of Laban raised high in the air, protecting the flocks of King Lamoni at the waters of Sebus. He revered his grandfather.

Ammon raised his hand and waved as he saw Nathan coming through the field.

The cow seemed to obey every command from Ammon. He had that effect on animals of all kinds.

It seemed every time trouble came, he was there to lead and help, whether runaway cows or skinned knees or just a story of days gone by. He was kind and loving, very much Christ-like.

His grandpa put his hand on Nathan's shoulder and said with a grin, "Guess what I found in that patch of weeds by the road?

"Can we sell her to the next merchant going to Zarahemla?" he asked cunningly, knowing that even if this old cow was a pain to keep in the fence, she gave plenty of milk for his family to enjoy.

Ammon said, "Maybe we should put a wooden yoke on her neck, and she won't be able to get through the fence. Let's ask your father. I also need to ask your father something else."

"What's that?" Nathan asked.

"Oh, if you can go to Zarahemla with me next week. You are twelve years old. I think it would be a great trip for you."

"Wow." Nathan's heart almost leaped out of his chest, and a thousand thoughts rushed through his mind.

Zarahemla was like another world, the buildings, the people, the merchants selling their wares, different food—everything a young boy could imagine.

His next question was, "Can Aaron and Joel come with us, Grandpa?"

"Yes, if their parents agree."

After some pleading, the parents agreed, all three boys could accompany Ammon to Zarahemla. They would leave next week.

# CHAPTER 7

## *A Trip to Remember*

Early the next week Ammon called for Nathan. His mother packed some food; clothes; and a short knife, which made him feel so grown-up. He kissed his mother and hugged his father. The girls were still asleep. As he strode out into the dark, he could see the silhouette of Aaron and Joel in the fading moonlight.

They would walk to Zarahemla, which was no big thing. They walked everywhere, and this would be fun having his cousins along to share every adventure with them. It was a three-day journey, which would take them along the coastline one day. They were to stay the night in a small village. The road headed southwest over the mountains through a pass and into a valley. The second night's stop was the top of the pass with guards from the army that guarded this part of the road leading to Zarahemla. In their company were two young men—one named Samuel and the other Helaman.

As this trip to remember started, Nathan strapped on his knife, feeling like a soldier. Ammon wore a sword and a bow with a quiver of arrows. Helaman carried a sword. Samuel held a long spear and a sword.

They all shouldered a pack made of skins and a water pouch. The morning went by quickly as everything was new and exciting. At noon, they stopped on a bluff overlooking a sandy beach. The sea stretched as far as a young boys' eyes could see.

Everyone found a seat under some small scrub trees that grew on the bluff and ate their noonday meal. Nathan lay on his back and stared up at the clouds. The sun was warm but not hot. A gentle breeze blew in from the ocean. He could smell the salty mist in the air. His grandfather closed his eyes and rested.

Joel and Aaron poked a stick in a nearby anthill and threw rocks off the bluff. They relaxed for a time. On no specific command, the men stood up, gathered their packs, and, with a nod of the head, all started in single file.

Winding their way along the bluff, always south, late in the afternoon, the young boys could see a village built in a cove back among the trees. Smoke was coming out of several huts, and they could see small boats tied to a dock and nets strung on poles along the beach.

The village set back in a grove of pine trees. It looked like a hundred or more buildings. Beyond the buildings, there were cleared fields with crops with sheep and cattle grazing. A very peaceful setting.

Ammon spoke. "We will stay with a very close friend of mine tonight. Be on your best behavior and manners."

It was almost dark when they entered the village. Families were cooking their evening meal, and children were playing, in the streets. Chickens and dogs ran here and there. Most people waved as the company came down the road. When word spread that Ammon was in the village, a great crowd began to gather at the home of the honored guests.

The company came to the front of the house. Several children jumped and ran inside, noisily chattering about the company of travelers that just arrived. A well-built, stout-looking man appeared in the doorway. His round face burst into a sunshine smile. He rushed with open arms to embrace Ammon. The feeling seemed mutual as they hugged and laughed, patted each other's backs, as tears rolled down their cheeks.

Nathan's grandfather beamed with happiness. Samuel and Helaman both rushed forward, sharing hugs all around, backslapping, tears, and much joy.

Nathan, Joel, and Aaron stood silent among this hardy welcome.

After a few minutes, things settled down and Ammon said in a rather loud voice, "Alma, I want you to meet my grandson, Nathan. Aaron and Joel, my brothers' grandsons."

Nathan's mouth dropped open. He was standing next to the prophet of God. His palms were sweaty, and his mouth dry. He knew all about Alma and who he was—a dear friend to his grandfather. To meet him was more than Nathan could ever hope. Alma was slightly shorter than Ammon. He had bright blue eyes that danced with light and sparkled with joy. He had broad shoulders and a kind, yet firm, face. He was saintly looking. He had large hands and strong arms, a high forehead, and dark-brown hair. He embraced Nathan, Joel, and Aaron with his massive arms, swallowing them in a hug. The boys just smiled and looked down as if looking at the prophet was going to hurt their eyes.

Alma then spoke. "Boys, I am delighted that you are here with your grandfather. My joy is so full to see my best friends in all the world."

Nathan stared at Alma and then at Helaman. It seemed that they were twins except one was older and one was younger. Still, they looked almost the same. He would ask his grandfather about it later.

Shortly, a gray-haired lady came out in the yard and announced food was ready.

Everyone needed to come inside, Nathan suddenly realized how hungry he was. He gave a sigh of praise to this woman that would feed the travelers tonight. They were led into a long pavilion with a table that filled the room with stools on each side. Large green leaves served as a placemat. Bowls of steaming food were placed on the table, fruit, vegetables, and meats prepared with care. There were fish from the sea and large pots of liquid. It looked so delicious.

Everyone gathered around the table. Alma stood and said a prayer. The feast commenced. Nathan, Aaron, and Joel sat together near the end of the table and began trying most of the food as it passed around. The boys ate and listened until they could eat no more.

Soon they realized how tired they were. An older grandmotherly woman came and motioned for them to follow. They stumbled along to a small hut near the eating place. Inside were mats and covers for each boy. They quickly got ready and were asleep instantly, dreaming of great adventures and heroic deeds.

# CHAPTER 8

## *The Great Walled City*

Nathan was up early the next morning. Aaron and Joel slept later and woke to the smell of breakfast. Nathan wandered into the village and watched it come to life—fisherman leaving with nets loaded in their boats, farmers heading out to work in the fields, children were walking toward a building in the middle of the village. He absorbed all the sights and sounds when his grandfather was suddenly standing next to him.

"Papa, this is such a lovely place, almost perfect in every way."

"Yes," Ammon said, "there is a peaceful feeling here."

They walked in silence for a while.

Nathan asked, "Will it always be like this?"

"No," came the reply. "There are dark days ahead. Trials are coming that will test all of us."

"What do you mean by that, Grandfather?"

"I mean, stay true to those lessons your mother is teaching you. Have faith in Christ, and always listen to the Spirit of God."

They walked on toward the longhouse.

"How will I recognize that Spirit?"

"From the feelings in your heart and the thoughts in your mind. It is a still small voice, but if you listen, you can hear the prompting."

*****

The group ate a quick breakfast, loaded the packs, and lined out to the far pass across the beautiful valley. The company would sleep tonight with the guards on the pass watching the road the next day. In the afternoon, they would enter Zarahemla, the largest city in the nation. The day was warm and sunny. Hiking was pleasant through the fields and trees. The smells of summer were everywhere. A small stream gurgled down the valley, and birds rose off the brook and landed in the nearby fields. The road passed by a large lake and headed into the forest as they began to climb to the pass.

Nathan, Aaron, and Joel dawdled but soon caught up as the company stopped for lunch. The woods were refreshing. The boys sat and ate their meal with visions of the city they would see tomorrow in their minds. Each boy imagined very different scenes in that great city Zarahemla.

The afternoon hike was uphill and required a lot of energy to keep up with the men. By the time the sun was setting in the west, young legs were heavy and dragging, as the company climbed the final incline and came out on a flat mesa.

Four guard huts surrounded a huge firepit, and two towers stationed at the edge of this little flat spot—one facing east, the other west. About twenty troops occupied this pass. More were placed here from time to time when they were needed. The guards received word that Ammon and his party would stay the night with them. A fine roasting fire was crackling and snapping. A small goat hung on a spit roasting. The man in charge of cooking was slowly turning the goat and basting it with a liquid.

The smell drifted toward the boys. As they unloaded their packs in the largest hut, which was big enough for all the company. Beds were on the ground made of firs and blankets. They each chose a spot, dropped their packs, and went to supper. There were big bowls of steaming vegetables, corn, and fruit served with large chunks of roasted goat folded in traditional flatbread. Washed down with sweet juice from a small round fruit collected in the forests and mixed with water, it was very refreshing. The hungry boys ate with gusto. They were listening to every word, laughing and talking with a mouth full of food, and having the most fabulous time of their young lives.

When the meal was finished and cleared away, the whole company headed straight to bed.

*****

Just as the sun peaked over the far mountains to the east, a gentle hand shook the boys one at a time. They stretched, yawned, rubbed the sleep from their eyes and came somewhat alive. Staggering out to a washing bowl and dipped their hands into the cold wash water and scrubbed their faces. Quickly dressing and packing their bundles, a hot pot of portage became breakfast. They said a prayer and moved out. The company was in a jovial mood this morning, joking, pushing, and shoving. It was a fun atmosphere, each excited about going to Zarahemla.

The morning passed quickly. The closer to the city, the more carts and wagons loaded with farm produce they saw heading toward the market. Passing a patrol of soldiers en route to relieve the troops at the pass. In the early afternoon, they entered an area where small farm homes dotted the landscape and fields on each side of the road. The stream that wound down from the hills grew into a more massive river where flatboats loaded with goods of all kinds moved along with the help of strong-looking horses.

In the distance, the great walled city appeared on the horizon. The boys stopped and gasped with excitement. There it was, Zarahemla!

# Chapter 9

## A Taste of Zarahemla

Nathan, Aaron, and Joel stood with their mouths gaping open. What a sight. They had only dreamed of this city, but now they were here. Samuel led the company through the many carts and people in a smooth flow toward the high gates that was opened for passage into the city.

Never had the boys seen such a high wall. It must have been thirty feet and about six feet thick. It was built of stone and plaster cement. The gates were massive. Wood logs shaped to fit together so close that Nathan thought they had grown together in the forest before someone cut them to use for this gate. Sentries stood on the wall lined along as far as Nathan could see.

Zarahemla divided into three main parts, three tiers or levels. As you pass through the gates, a soldier in a bright red coat stopped everyone and asked for their name, business in the city, and where they were staying. The bottom level, the market place, shops lined the streets. Outdoor canopies divided each merchant and his wares. There seemed to be an order to this massive shopping center. Cloth and clothing, rugs, furs, leather, ropes, and a million other items lined one side of the market.

The other aisle was foodstuff of all kinds of fish, meat, vegetables, fruit, grain, and bread. Every imaginable thing a young boy could think of was here. Swords, spears, knives, clubs, and shields—everything to outfit an army. Horses and donkeys pulled the carts. Dogs darted in and out of the people's feet, looking for a scrap of meat. Chickens roosted along the rails of the fences. The sights were amazing, and the smells brought the boys toward the food. What smelled so good? They didn't quite know. Still, they wanted to find out. The company slowed, and the three boys moved into the front, mouths gaped open, moving toward the food market.

Ammon reached out and touched Nathan's arm. "Would you like to try something new from this market?"

"Yes, yes, we would," came the reply.

"Okay, follow me. I will give a taste of Zarahemla." Ammon gathered the three boys around.

The rest of the company bid the boys good-bye and went to their homes. Still, the sights and smells of the market place were so real and enticing. The boy's mouths watered as they stood gawking at all the little shops and cookeries. Ammon showed the boys to a large covered pavilion and whispered something to an older woman with a head full of gray hair, looking very spry.

She hopped along like her legs wanted to go faster than her body. Her wrinkled face stretched when she smiled, and she smiled a lot. Jumping right over to the boys, she grabbed them by the hands and sat them down on a thick chair with a high back and a pillow on the seat.

First, she brought a large bowl of hot water and soft towels. Her voice was rather squawky, high pitched, full of love, and care. She told the boys, "You wash first, then I feed you the best dinner in Zarahemla."

They plunged hands and faces into the water, blowing and sputtering, the water felt good after the dusty road dirt and sweat that covered their faces and hands, arms, and hair. After washing exercises were over, they said a quiet prayer led by Aaron. Young ladies a few years older than the boys brought large wooden bowls of food. There was meat on long sticks cooked over the open fire. Fowl was split down the back and spread out, roasted with a red past. There were long yellow squash, corn roasted in a pit, fish cooked with the skin crispy and tasty, bread and fruit, and a smooth brown drink that was soooo flavorful.

They ate until they could eat no more, then laughed and giggled with the young ladies. They gazed at the night lights and the stars and finally realized how tired they were.

Ammon stood up and said, "Let's go to my home. We will sleep there tonight."

The house they went to was Ammon's childhood home where he lived with his brothers and his father, King Mosiah, and his mother on the third level of the city. The homes here were close together but private because of the wall around the perimeter. A garden was just inside the wall. The house had three levels. A large family room and kitchen on the first floor with a washroom. The second floor divided into six smaller rooms with bedding and pillows, places to hang clothes, windows to view the streets of the city. The third level was part large dining room and an open-air area to visit or have some quiet time away from the bustle of the town. It was very comfortable and cozy.

Nathan felt the peace that rested there. He was led to a sleeping room and fell asleep in ten minutes. Aaron and Joel joined him. They were asleep, dreaming of the many wonders of this big city. Ammon's family maintained the home, his father having passed away many years before. It was also very close to the temple and the government buildings where the chief judge spent his day governing the land.

The next morning the boys were awakened by the sound of movement on the bottom floor. They tossed and wrestled in the bedding with each other.

Washed and dressed in clean clothes, they tumbled down the stairs to be greeted by their traveling companions.

Ammon stood and spoke. "Boys, today will be a day to remember for the rest of your lives, so be calm and respectful."

# CHAPTER 10

## *Sacred Things*

The mood was somber among the group. Helaman wore a purple tunic with a vest of leather. Ammon had white with a red sash. Ammon told the boys to stay close and listen. The young boys stared into space, not knowing what any of this meant. Helaman led Samuel and Ammon. The kids followed along as they moved out into the street and up the hill.

Their first stop was a tall round building with large stones making up the foundation and walls, a rounded roof made of wood and shingle, windows on all sides, and a large door pointing out toward the street. As they were walking into the building, Nathan noticed a large room with a round table in the center and seated at the table were a group of distinguished-looking men.

Ammon and Helaman began shaking hand and slapping the men on the back. Each stood and gave reverence to Ammon. Nathan saw the respect these men had for his grandfather. A lump came to his throat, and tears welled up in his eyes. Whoever these men were, they loved his grandfather and were seeking his counsel.

Ammon turned and said, "Brothers, let me introduce to you Joel, the grandson of my brother Omner. This is Aaron, my brother Aaron's grandson, and this is Nathan, my grandson."

A tall man with a chiseled face and broad shoulders stood and faced them. He had a full head of thick dark hair cropped short, large brown eyes, and a sharp nose with a kind smile. A steady hand shot out, and a voice that commanded respect spoke.

"I am Captain Moroni."

Nathan stood in utter disbelief. His eyes blinked wide. Before him stood the leader of the Nephite army, the man who raised the Title of Liberty. His mouth opened, but nothing came out. Nathan stuck his hand out and felt the strength in this man's hand. Finally, he squawked out something and ducked his head. Awkward as it was for him, he didn't want to release the handshake.

A shorter, slight, more intense man with sharp, hawk-like eyes stood. He was surveying all that was going on before him, a stern expression on his face. "I am Teancum, defender of right."

Nathan took his hand and felt a surge of energy from this warrior.

Next, he met Lehi and Antipus, both great leaders in the Nephite army.

A younger-looking man put his hand on Nathan's shoulder and spoke in a calm yet grim voice. "I am Pahoran." He pointed to an older, distinguished-looking man. "This is my father, Nephihah."

Helaman took his seat along with Samuel and two other captains.

This council sat in a circle, twelve men in all, speaking low and quiet to each other.

The boys took a seat off to the side and watched as the council came to order.

Ammon said a prayer. Captain Moroni stood and reached for a map with marks in black, red, and green.

As the meeting progressed, each person took a turn speaking.

Nathan knew nothing of the council, just that it concerned the Nephite nation. The grave expressions of these leaders marked how serious they were.

Two hours later, the men all stood and bid each other farewell.

Ammon motioned to the boys to follow him, and off they went out the side door leading to the temple, which sat on a raised hill about five hundred yards from the round building. Ammon entered first and gathered the boys around and said, "Take off your shoes and follow me."

He led them down a hallway around the corner into a room with a large wooden door that closed after them. Soon the door opened. Helaman came in carrying a carved wooden box. In the corner of the room was a small table and several shelves with scrolls and metal plates and tablets of all kinds. Helaman set the box on the table and removed the cloth covering the box carved with several strange images.

Ammon stepped forward. "Boys, I am going to show you something sacred and ancient." He raised the lid on the box. "These are the brass plates that Nephi took from Laban and brought back to his father, Lehi, the patriarch of our family."

Each boy knew this story by heart. They knew of the teachings of the brass plates from their lessons in school and the stories told to them each night by their mothers as they prepared for bed.

Right in front of them lay the actual plates, not a copy, but the real thing. All they could do was look. They did not touch them. Each young man felt a still small voice whisper to them, "This is real, and the teachings on these plates are right." A warm feeling came into their hearts they had not felt before.

After about five minutes, Ammon closed the lid on the box.

Helaman said, "Boys, look here." In his hands lay a sword in a leather sheath. The hilt was gold with jewels, and the blade was like a silver light unleashed in a dark room. "This is the Sword of Laban."

The boys also knew the story of this sword and the power it possessed. Ammon carried it at the waters of Sebus. Still, they just stared at it shining in Helaman's hand.

Ammon, lead the boys down a long hall, which entered into a larger round room with benches around the out sidewalls. He said, "Sit down. Let me tell why I wanted you to see these brass plates. In them is the genealogy of our family—the words of the prophets. In years to come, you will have the blessing to protect this nation and stand as a witness for the great Jehovah, as your grandfathers and fathers have done. It's important you know they are real. If necessary, give your lives for the truths they teach. Listen to your mothers as they guide you."

Nathan whispered, "Grandfather, I feel a warm feeling inside. What is that?"

"That is the Holy Ghost telling you these things are true."

Sitting in the temple, each boy felt the prompting. What they witnessed was sacred. It became a living testimony of the scriptures, how important they are to the Nephite nation.

Aaron spoke in a hushed tone. "Nephi was not much older than us when he got the plates. Could we do something like that?"

Joel looked up. "I am not sure. If we did it together, we could."

Ammon stood and motioned with his hand. The young men followed out the door and into the street.

Nathan observed, "It's a different feeling outside the temple."

"Yes, it is." Ammon smiled. "It is the house of the Lord."

As the day came to an end, the boys were fatigued by this spiritual outpouring. They stumbled home, ate a quick meal, and fell into bed with visions of mighty deeds of valor and swords of righteous power, slaying all who opposed them in their dreams.

# CHAPTER 11

# *Why Would God Do This to Me?*

The boys woke hungry ready for breakfast. Ammon called to them to get ready and come down to the kitchen. They moved quickly to wash and dress after a meal of bread and cheese with fruit. A young man arrived at the house.

"This is your guide for the day. His name is Levi," Grandpa said. "I will be busy for the next two days. Levi will show you the whole city."

They ran through the streets; climbed the wall; revisited the marketplace several times, watching the merchants unload fresh meat, fruit, grain, fish, cloth, and many other items to sell at the market. They spent time watching the garrison of soldiers drill in the morning sun and went swimming in a river in the afternoon. They ate supper under the stars with Levi's family. What an exciting adventure for the boys. They even took time to discuss and ponder what sacred events they witnessed in the Temple. This trip to the capital city was an education for the three striplings. It was something to be remembered for the rest of their lives, with feelings planted deep in their hearts for the scriptures on the brass plates. They experienced wonderful friends, excellent food, and a time of growing into young men, which would bond the boys even closer.

\*\*\*\*\*

Sometimes it takes years to understand why things happen as they do, and in the end, only God knows for sure why.

On this ordinary morning, Heth kissed Naomi, Ruth, and Sariah good-bye and grabbed his tool bag and water jug. He was off to help a newly arrived family build a home on the outskirts of the little village just north of the main road. It was a beautiful plot of ground for this family. It had good soil for a garden, water in a creek, trees scattered across the meadow to the back—everything the family would need to make a comfortable home and begin a new life with the people of Ammon.

The outside walls of the house were in place. It was now time to place a ridge pole at the top of the ridge. On each end wall, at the top, a notch was left big enough for a ridge pole to fit. The pole was the length of the house. Rafters would be fastened from the ridge pole to the walls every two feet. Then long shingles boards were horizontally installed over the beams, making a watertight roof.

This morning was wet and muddy. Raining most of the night left the dirt floor a mud pit. Several men showed up to help lift the huge log into place. Heth moved the ladders into position. The plan was to secure one end in the pocket, and then ropes and levers lift the other end and slide it in place and cut off the excess. Everything went as planned. The first end slipped in the pocked with not much trouble. A stubborn knot overlooked on the pole would not fit. Everyone shoved it. On the muddy soil, the ladders slipped. The massive log dropped, shooting logs everywhere and slamming to the ground. Heth, standing on the ladder, tried to steady the pole but caught the full weight directly on top of his head, crushing him to the ground and pinning him under the log. Men rushed to lift the pole off Heth. It took several minutes to move the massive pole. Carefully, he was loaded into a cart and taken home to Sariah. She met the men in the front yard, Namoi and Ruth at her side.

Heth opened his eyes. "I love you, my girls." Breathing came shallow. His eyes closed, and he grimaced in pain. "Sariah, take care of our family. Tell Nathan I love him." He shifted a little. "Thanks for a great life. I love you, Sariah. We will be with Jesus someday." His eyes closed, and his once firm grip went limp.

Sariah whispered, "Good-bye, Heth, until we meet in paradise." She drew a blanket over his bruised body and brought the girls close and cried and prayed, "Please, God, help Nathan get through this tragedy."

*****

The next morning it was time to say good-bye to Zarahemla and journey back to Jershon. The company consisted of the three boys, Samuel, Helaman, Teancum, ten soldiers going to the pass, and Ammon. After an early breakfast, they were off at a brisk march, wanting to make the pass by night. It was necessary to move along at a steady pace. Teancum was in the lead, pushing forward at every point. The boys' legs were shaky and weak. At the first rest stop, they slumped to the ground and dozed off.

Too soon, someone nudged Nathan and said, "Son, it's time to go." He rolled over and stood up. Surprisingly, he felt refreshed and ready.

They lined out again and moved through a forest of trees and started the climb up into the mountains. By late afternoon, the company topped out at the pass and covered the last mile to the fort.

Dragging along, the boys sat down and removed their packs. Everyone was busy getting ready for the night and the evening meal. Teancum took three soldiers and disappeared over the pass and moved toward the valley below.

Just as dinner was ready, he reappeared, sat, and ate with everyone.

After dinner, Teancum and Ammon visited in low hushed tones away from the fire. When Ammon came back to the boys, he was weeping and somber. He called Nathan over to him and put his arm around him and gave him a tight squeeze. He said, "Please sit down."

Nathan's knees almost buckled. "What is it, Grandfather? What's happened?"

Ammon wiped his eyes and said, "It's your father, Nathan. He is dead."

The words hit the young man like a club. He lost all of his breath, his head was dizzy, and he fell face down on the earth. Getting to his knees, he finally found enough air to speak.

"What happened?" he shouted. "No, no, it can't be. He's home with my family."

Ammon said, "I know how hard this is, my son. Your father was helping a new family build a house. As they were putting the ridge pole up for the roof, it slipped and crushed him under it. He passed away about two hours later in the arms of your mother. His burial was three days ago. Teancum met a messenger tonight."

Ammon sat with his arms around Nathan for over an hour as his young body shook with great sobs, a whimpering sound escaping between great gulps of air. Nathan loved his father, and he knew his father loved him. He also knew that there was nothing that his father would not do for him. He was Nathan's hero and example. Now he was gone, all Nathan could say was, "Why would God do this to me?"

Ammon did not answer him right then, just held him and shared the grief that comes from losing someone you love. Sometime later that night, both crawled into bed and slept for a few hours.

The next morning Aaron and Joel came and sat, talking to Nathan. The cousins were as close as brothers. Tears burst from all three.

It was two full days of travel on foot to reach home, so off they went. Aaron and Joel took turns packing Nathan's pack. As one of the men tried to haul the backpack, they said, "No, we can do this for our brother."

That day three young men grew more toward being who they would become in the years that followed. Nathan was silent and stunned. He drank only a little water and ate just a few bites of food.

The next night the company stayed at the village where they lodged on the trip to Zarahemla. It was a solemn night. The boys sat together, Aaron on one side and Joel on the other with Nathan in the middle. They peered into the fire and spoke seldom. Tears came at times. The cousins were grieving together. Heartfelt hugs were genuine. Aaron and Joel felt love for Nathan. It was hard to watch someone who had always been happy and lively so sad and depressed. It broke their hearts and were at a loss as to what to say or do. So they just sat together and gave the only thing they could—love. Not some romance type love that young men shy away from, but caring and feeling for others, trying to help ease the grief and pain caused by the loss of a loved one. The night passed, and morning came. The company moved out.

As the boys were getting started, Ammon said, "Today we ride. We need to be home tonight," as several horses appeared, saddled and ready for the trek. Helaman, Ammon, and the three boys mounted the horses. The others in the company left an hour before and were going in a different direction. The boys did know how to ride. It's just that they walked almost everywhere. The horses were a welcome sight to tired legs. Off they headed in a rapid canter, going home to face the situation of a life without a father.

# CHAPTER 12

## *A Time of Growing*

As Nathan rode up to his house, his mother came running out to greet him. Sariah threw her arms around her son and squeezed him so tight, he lost all of his breath. She patted his back and cupped his face in her hands. The flood of tears came. Ammon slid off his horse and joined the family hug. His daughter was hurting. He wanted to comfort and love her.

Sariah looked into his face and said, "Dad, how can I do this without Heth? How can I go on? It's so hard."

Tears streamed down the man of God's face. His soul grieved for his daughter. He knew the raw pain of losing your best friend and eternal companion. Ammon himself experienced that loss several years ago in the land of Ishmael. Heth committed to serve God that fateful day when he and Sariah made a pact with God to share the rest of their lives. Ammon's sweet spouse lost her life to the wicked Lamanites that day. His life changed forever as he came to know the meaning of forgiveness differently and the comfort the Holy Ghost brings to one that suffers unbearable pain.

As he stood holding his daughter and grandson, the memories flooded back and the feelings of loneliness and the love his Savior has for those who suffer the loss of one so dear.

"We will grieve together, we will grow together, we will worship together, and the Eternal Father in heaven will make us whole again."

Nathan felt anger growing in his breast and his mind. He couldn't understand how a God that loves his children could let

63

something so terrible happen to such good people. He shouted a little too loud, "Grandpa, why, why, why?" He stuttered through sobs of grief.

Ammon took his grandson by his shoulders and looked into his wet bloodshot eyes and said, "Son, I read something many years ago written by the great prophet, Nephi. It goes something like this, 'I do not know the meaning of all things, but I do know that God loves his children.' Someday we will see the purpose of these events in our lives, but for now, we must live by the faith that God knows us and knows what we need to bring us closer to him."

Nathan said, "I have never felt further away from God than right now."

"Let's make it through this day, and we will face tomorrow and the next day and the next day and so on, seeking the understanding to see as God sees, to feel as he feels."

"I will try," Nathan sighed. "I will try." His mind was numb.

A gray cloud consumed Nathan's thoughts for a few days. Anger gave way to despair. He didn't want to get out of bed. Sariah let him lay in bed for a couple of days.

The next morning she came in very early. It was still dark outside. She shook Nathan until he woke. He sat up, rubbing the sleep from his red bloodshot eyes.

He moaned, "What's wrong?"

"Nothing, son. I want you to come to take a walk with me. It will do us both good."

"Mom, I don't feel like walking."

"I know, but we're going to do it anyway."

"What are we doing?"

"You are going to see what your father did for the people of this village. Put this shoulder harness."

Out the back door of Nathan's house was a two-wheeled cart filled with bags of flour, bread, produce from the garden, meat from the storage room, woven cloth, leather shoes—things a family would need to start a new life in a new land.

"Where did all this come from?"

"Your father not only helped most people build a home as they moved into this land. He would make sure they had enough to eat and clothes to wear while getting settled. He left this early in the morning to get back to his work during the day."

"Where are we going?" Nathan whined.

A deep voice behind him in the dark spoke up. "Down at the central gathering place a group of people came in yesterday. We will help them get settled this morning."

"But, Grandpa, can't someone else help them this time?"

"No," Ammon said. "It's our turn, so let's go."

Nathan and Ammon pulled the loaded cart, and Sariah pushed. It would take an hour to reach the gathering place and another to unload this food and goods and another hour back home. Sweat and hard work, does wonder for sorrow.

After three trips in one week, Nathan asked his mother, "Mom, how do you keep going?"

Stopping for a short drink of water and rest, she said, "Son, I have faith that God needed my husband with him more than we needed him here. I know that Jesus Christ will overcome death. We will be together as a family again. That's what keeps me going every day. I miss your father every day, and I miss my mother. I have felt the loving comfort of the Spirit. That's what you must do. Have faith that Christ will help you understand and feel that all things will work for our good."

Longing to see his father again, Nathan crawled out of bed, half kneeled, half crouched on the floor, and cried out to God, "If you can hear me, God, answer me why my father had to die." He lay there, sobbing, crying, and questioning.

After what seemed like hours, Nathan floated off into a dream. It seemed real and vivid. He was standing on a rise overlooking a street. People were kneeling in the street with hands raised toward heaven praising God. Two figures with their backs toward him were bent over someone lying on the road. The people never looked up, but great sobs racked their body, and a sadness hung over the scene like a dark cloud.

A voice spoke to Nathan. "Your mother and grandfather lost someone they loved long ago. You can receive strength from them."

A calm feeling rested on the young man. He slipped back into bed. The healing process began. Somehow he would make his father proud.

For now, Nathan knew three things—one, life was hard; two, his mother and grandfather loved him; and three, work was not all that bad.

A few days later, while gathering eggs, with his mother, he said, "I had a dream. I saw grandma lying on the road and grandpa crying by her side. And you were there also. How do you know grandma and our dad are alive with God?"

"Nathan, look at this egg. What's inside it?"

"A yolk and white."

"How do you know that?"

"Mom, I've seen lots of eggs, and everyone has a yolk in it."

"So you have faith that this one also does?"

"Yes, I suppose."

"Did the sun come up today?"

"Yes, it did."

"Will it come up tomorrow?"

"Yes, I believe it will."

"The God who put the yolk inside this egg and caused the sun to rise every day of your life has said his only begotten son, Jesus Christ, would come to earth to pay for our sins and to overcome death so all of his children can return and live with him again. Nathan, Christ knows how you feel losing your father, and if you can believe the sun will rise tomorrow and every egg will have a yolk, then believe that Jesus Christ will make all things right. For now, have faith."

"Mom, that sounds so easy, but it seems so hard. I believe everything you say, Mom, because I know you teach me the truth."

# CHAPTER 13

## *Becoming a Young Man*

Nathan's next few weeks were full of grief and doubt. He questioned his faith. He felt scared and despised his life. Finally, he came to understand his sisters were hurting just as bad as he was. Namoi and Ruth needed his love. They also lost their father.

In a sullen voice, he said, "Namoi, Ruth, I am sorry the way I have acted. I thought I was the only one grieving. I came to realize I have neglected you both through this ordeal. You also must be hurting inside. Can you forgive me? I do love you and want to be a family forever. I'll try being better. We can heal together."

He became a real older brother, treating them with love and respect. Nathan looked outside himself to those he loved the most. He helped with the garden, gave Namoi a break from milking the cow, and hauled firewood for Ruth. He washed the dishes for his mother and carried water for drinking and cooking.

Service to his family made him happy. Nathan found the cure for all his despair—work, backbreaking work, every day. And a game that took Nathan's mind off his grief.

He farmed the fields. It was time to plant. Heth prepared all the fields before he passed. Now it was Nathan's duty to plant the crops to feed his family for the next year. Helping his father for the last three years, Nathan knew what to do. It wouldn't be as good as his dad's planting, but he could do it. They always saved seeds from the last year for farming. Heth stored the grain in large clay jars, dry and safe from any rodents. Nathan knew now why he spent time putting seed in the jars last year and sealing them.

Aaron and Joel came to help just as the sun came over the horizon. Each filled their bags with seeds and down the rows with a spade in one hand, digging a shallow hole, dropping in seeds and moving on. They planted corn, beans, peas, squash, several vegetables, wheat, oats, and several different grains. It took two full days to plant all the fields to mark each plot and record the day and times. Aaron and Joel from start to finish helped Nathan. It always made the boys feel close to each other.

Jershon, being close to the sea, was well-watered. It rained at least once every week. Plants grew quickly and fast. The weather was hot in the days and cool at night, perfect for fruit, vegetables, grains, and gardens.

Ammon came by one morning and said, "Today, I am going to teach you a game we played when I was a boy growing up in Zarahemla. I played with all my brothers and our friends. Even Alma played this game. We called it old sow. It's rough but great fun if you survive. Gather all the kids in the neighborhood. Make sure Aaron and Joel come, and meet me this afternoon out in that cow pasture behind the corals Bring a thick tree limb as big as your arm, as long as your leg, one for each boy. Also, bring a spade."

Nathan scratched his head. "I'll be there."

Yes, just after the sun passed the high point of the day, twelve boys with clubs all about the same size gathered at the cow pasture at Nathan's invitation. Ready for whatever came, Ammon came carrying a small round ball of leather, tightly bound together, about the size of a large apple. It is called the pig or the ball. He took the spade and dug eleven shallow holes deep as a man's hand in a twenty-foot circle. Next, Ammon dug a hole in the middle of the ring.

"Now each boy except Aaron gets a hole to protect. Aaron will be the old sow. The object of this game is to move the leather ball with your stick along, trying to put it in someone's hole. If you do, you must step on it and shout, 'One, two, three old sow.' If the person can't get it out of his hole with his stick, he becomes the old sow. The person who is the old sow moves the leather pig along. Anyone can sneak out of his hole and knock the pig away into the pasture. If a hole is left empty, it is free for the taking. Whoever ends up without a hole is the old sow. If the old sow person gets the pig in the center hole and cries, 'Old sow,' he can call any player to be the old sow."

With that explanation, the game began, and oh, what a game. Cracked shins, smashed fingers, pounded toes. What a great match. Three hours later, after some blood, sweat, and a few tears, old sow was dubbed the official game of all the young men of Jershon. Word spread fast about the new game. Any spare time the boys could find and an open field, the fight was on. The river boys played the farmers. The village kids played the hill country youth. It was such a passion that even young ladies played. Families clubbed each other in friendly games.

The most determined game players were the future stripling warriors. Little did they realize this game would prepare them for real-life battles in the not-so-distant future. For now, it was to show their manhood and tear up the ground.

The next morning Sariah stopped, looked at Nathan, and said, "Son, what happened to your hand? It's all red and scabbed and you're limping. Do you have a hurt foot?"

"Yeah, Mom, it's the best game ever Grandpa showed us. See, you get these sticks and you have these holes and a leather ball, and someone tries to put the ball in your hole, and you knock it out with your stick. And sometimes you miss and hit his leg or his hand. See my hand right here"—he pointed to his bruised knuckles—"Joel got me here. And the new kid from over by the road his family came two weeks ago, he was feeling a little alone, well he whacked me on the leg. It hurt, but wow, it was fun. We're planning a game again tomorrow after everyone gets their work done, if that's all right with you?"

"And what do you call this?"

"Old sow. Would you come and watch us?"

"Yes, with a bag full of bandages and a pot full of my green salve."

"Thanks, Mom."

The green salve came from a receipt handed down to Sariah from her mother. Many generations of women gathered roots, plants, seeds and bark that grew in the region. In making this salve, all the ingredients were mashed between a large rectangular smooth rock and a large flat cupped rock. After smashing everything together, it became a paste-like substance that possessed extreme healing power. This salve helped humans, cattle, goats, sheep, and young boys with wounds from old sow games. It later served a whole army to heal wounds received in real battles.

Nathan, Joel, and Aaron went hiking to the mountains. They fish in the rivers and told stories by the fires at night. And they played old sow with everyone that would play. It was proper medicine for grief and sorrow.

*****

The family worked hard all summer and gathered a bountiful harvest. The hand of the Lord blessed them in every way. An abundance of crops were stored for Nathan's family in their storage rooms while the reminder was sent a to the army that protected the borders of Jershon.

A spirit of love and comfort came to each family member. Joel and Aaron spent almost every day helping Nathan.

After the first harvest, the family settled into life without their father and husband. Life was somewhat typical—plant the fields, care for the animals.

Although there was not a lot of time to relax, the boys did enjoy spending time in the forest hunting and fishing, finding secret corners of the nearby country, and knocking the shins of each other while playing old sow.

Wandering through the farm country on the outskirts of Jershon, the three boys meet several farm kids engaged in a ferocious game of old sow. At the invitation of a short, sturdy young man, they joined the game. Finding a stick is the most important thing to accomplish when playing old sow. The bat needs to be light enough to move fast yet strong enough to withstand the blows of a charging old sow club wielder intent on getting your hole or moving the old sow ball into the hole.

Each boy chose a stick and joined the fun. They knew most of these boys from the market in Jershon when the farmers brought their produce or livestock to sell or trade. The game was in progress. It seemed to be controlled by the short fellow. His name was Joseph, and he had no problem smashing ankles or toes with a chuckle and off after the ball, swinging wildly at anything in his way.

Joel, usually a quiet, calm sort of kid, caught a club on his right shin as the pig cantered off a stick. Joseph just kept swinging. Another smack to Joel's leg and it bled a little. It swelled up in a humongous bump halfway up his leg. That was it. He grabbed Joseph's stick, jerked it from his hands, and threw it across the field. He grabbed him in a headlock, and down to the ground they went. Joel was on top, and Joseph was struggling to get loose.

"You have hit me for the last time. You think everyone will back off if you swing that club and beat their legs. Well, you are not doing that to me again."

The game stopped, and everyone stood in a circle looking at the boys in the dirt. One was kicking wildly to get loose. The other locked in a death grip of a headlock, not giving an inch. The struggling stopped. Joseph relaxed and said, "Okay, let me up."

Joel released the headlock, and the two combatants stood to face each other.

Nathan knew Joel as well as any brother. He had never seen this side of Joel. No anger, just a resolve. He was determined not to have this little warrior beat his shin to a bloody pulp. His jaw set in a firm pose, and his eyes bright and stern.

"You will play the game right, or I will take you down again and rub your face in the dirt."

Joseph blinked, shifted his feet, sizing up the boy who just pounded him into the ground. Being a happy-go-lucky, friendly young man, he shot his hand forward, grabbed Joel's hand, and asked sincerely, "Will you forgive me? I just love this combat so much I get carried away. Thanks for teaching me a lesson."

They shook hands, patted each other on the backs, and said, "Okay, let's play."

The game started again. Joseph was more in control of his stick, which made everybody playing at ease.

Joel picked up his stick and charged back into the fray. Nathan stared in amazement at his loveable cousin.

*****

The following week it was time to help the new families get settled. Nathan pulled the loaded cart into the square, stopped, and noticed he wasn't tired. He looked around and saw a small tent-looking structure made of two long pieces of heavy cloth tied together with string. Thrown over a rope between two trees served as a shelter for the last family here this morning. Everyone else had a relative or close friend to stay with until they could get settled. All the people went off to different parts of the country.

This family had almost nothing. A girl about the same age as Nathan's sister Namoi was bent over a fire with a single pot cooking a mush made of corn and barley flour. Another child was picking chips of wood under the trees to keep the light going while a woman sat holding a young boy, crying and dirty.

From sleeping on the ground, the whole family looked worn-out, traveling for at least five weeks, everything they owned crammed in one large wool bag. A small flour sack held all the food left from the five-week journey.

Gazing on this family, Sariah thought, *We have so much room. I could use the help around the farm, and the girls would love to have new friends.*

The cart rolled to a stop. Nathan spoke to the girl at the fire.

"Hello, my name's Nathan. What yours?"

Without looking up, she, squeaked, "Dianna."

"Are you hungry? I have cheese, bread, eggs, milk, meat, and some apples."

A bushy head shot up with interest in the invitation for a delicious breakfast. It looked straight into the most handsome face she could ever imagine. A little taken back by this cute stranger with an invitation for breakfast, she stuttered, "A-a-a…yes, we would like to eat."

Hearing the mention of fresh food other than mush, the rest of the family stood and came on a trot. Eating the same mush for the last week was unbearable.

Sariah stepped forward, introduced herself, and said, "This is my son, Nathan."

He stopped and did a full sweeping bow. "At your service."

Aza smiled. "Thank you, young man. I am Aza. These are my daughters, Dianna and Sara. And this is Asher, my son."

The three kids lined next to their mother and said, "At your service."

Nathan took over the cooking; and Sariah helped clean up the family, wash their faces, and beating the dirt out of the old blankets. A flat rock severed as a table. All stood around the stone, eating and talking.

Aza told of their conversion to the gospel, of the persecution in the land of Nephi. She and her husband decided to move the family to Jershon. He was forced into the Lamanite army and killed in a battle five years ago. They tried to survive when she heard other members were going with the people of Ammon. Aza sold all they owned to make the journey. Now they are in this new land, free to worship God without anything.

Sariah spoke. "You will come and live with us. My husband died, and I have a son and two daughters. Our house is large enough for two families, and our farm produces much more than we can use. Will you come and be a part of our family?"

Aza could only shake her head. Tears of gratitude streamed down her face. "Thank you."

Nathan loaded all their belongings in the cart, slung the harness over his shoulder, and put Asher and Sara in the cart.

He asked Dianna, "Would like to ride?"

"No," she said. "I want to walk by you." She looked into his brown eyes and smiled her sweetest smile.

Nathan felt more responsibilities to help feed and shelter this new family. He thought it an honor to help another family in similar circumstances as his own.

He decided when and how much to plant, how many animals to keep, how many to barter and trade. He enjoyed helping others. Since his father passed, Nathan found his purpose in life, service. As he grew, his love for others grew. The thought of helping others pleased him. This new family added to his overall happiness. He came to understand he was following in his father's footsteps. The house they lived in was large. Heth planned well as he built the home.

There was room for Aza and all the children. All settled into a routine that worked for both families. The children accepted tasks according to age. School was fun with more students, which Sariah oversaw. Aza did the cooking with Sara and Ruth. Dianna and Naomi cared for the animals. Everyone cleaned the house and washed the clothes. There were weeds to pull, bread to bake, and neighbors to help. It was a great life. Everyone in the house got along fine. Dianna thought Nathan was the cutest boy ever. On the other hand, Nathan only saw her as a little sister. Life moved on for the young lady, living so close to her dream yet not able to get noticed.

*****

Dianna and Naomi worked all summer getting the lambs ready for market. The girls possessed a natural talent to care for livestock. Now at almost sixteen, they were beautiful and quite smart about raising animals and farming. In the fall, merchants from Zarahemla came to Jershon to purchase livestock, and the girls were ready to go to the market. It turned into a celebration. Also, the harvest was mostly over. Everyone from the outlining area coming into the main village to trade and barter for tools and goods and to visit old friends.

Joseph and Benjamin came and stayed with Nathan. They would sell or barter their flocks. Spend a week in the city, as they called it, then head back to the country for the winter. The boys thought an old sow game was in order, and the girls asked if they could play. The boys, of course, considered this a time to show these girls how to play the game. Nathan, Aaron, Joel, Joseph, Benjamin, and Asher said, "If you can take it. There is no crying if you're hurt."

The girls—Dianna, Naomi Ruth, Sara, and Dawn, a girl from the market invited to come home and play—replied, "Does that mean for you, boys?"

It started with a circle with ten holes. Dianna became the old sow. She moved the pig toward Nathan's hole. He swung his stick. She checked it with her stick. *Clunk.* The sticks hit together. Joel snuck into Nathan's hole. Dianna scurried to get the vacant hole left void by Joel. Just as her stick reached the hole, Ruth's stuck her stick in the hole. Meantime, Joseph smacked the pig out in the field, and Nathan spun for Joseph's hole, only to find Dianna there first. She shoved him out of the way and crouched ready as Aaron, now the old sow, brought the pig back careful to protect it. With his club, Benjamin came forward and swung at the pig. He missed and hit Naomi in the leg. She squealed, raised her club, and thumped Benjamin on the knee. He hobbled back to an empty hole, howling like a sick cat. Dawn shoved Aaron with a hip movement, and an inside swing sent the pig rolling out in the tullywads. Aaron looked at this dark-haired beauty. Wow, this game took on a whole new twist. These girls knew how to play, and they weren't afraid to mix it up. He kind of liked that. Joel and Sara were pushing each other as the pig smacked Joel in the back of the head. He laughed and just kept pushing Sara. She just smiled and pushed back. Meanwhile, Dianna was having the time of her life.

Of all the things Nathan had overcome, Dianna confused him the most. She would work alongside him in the corrals in knee-deep muck, she chopped weeds and picked corn, she washed clothes and cared for the sheep and goats as good as any man. She could weave a rug and plant a field. And now she could play old sow like a boy!

Just then, he felt a slam to his solid two-hundred-pound frame. This mighty redhead gave him an elbow in the midsection and said, "If you are going to stand and watch, move over to the side. There is a game going on! Out of my way." And with that, she was off to an empty hole that Benjamin just vacated. Smiling sweetly at him, she said, "Sorry, big boy, did I hurt you?"

He rolled his eyes and tore into the brawl.

After two hours, the young participants called an end to the contest. They hobbled to the back door of Sariah's kitchen, washed off the dust, and enjoyed a sweet treat of fruit and cake under the night sky.

Female companionship was a new experience for the boys, and they liked it.

Nathan sat down next to Dianna, looking at her for the first time as a young lady. He was finding it difficult to talk to her for the first time since her family moved in with his family. Some strange feeling he was feeling for Dianna. Nathan always liked her, but now it was more caring, wanting to be near her. He looked into her face, trying to make her laugh, asking her opinion about anything so he could hear her talk. He sat next to her after the old sow game, eating a sweet small cake and enjoying being with all his friends.

Nathan asked, "Where did you learn to play old sow so well?"

She looked at him. "Nathan, this is me, Dianna. What do you mean where did I learn to play old sow so well? We've played several times, or didn't you notice?"

He felt stupid. Of course, she had played many times, but not like this, as a real girl.

He said, "Oh, yeah. Dianna, do you like living with our family?" Nathan was now more serious.

She paused for a long time and then began, "Your family is so kind to us to provide a home and place to live. We love all of you for your kindness. We would not want to live anyplace else.

"Dianna, what will you do in a few years?"

"Why do you ask, Nathan?"

His face went bright red, and he stammered, "Just wondering."

She knew she had him in a tight place. He was serious, and she was ready to tease him a little. "Oh, I thought you were proposing marriage or something."

"Would you be grown-up for a minute," he puffed.

Dianna contorted her face into a prune, and in her best impression of him, said. "I would like to marry a wealthy farmer and have ten children and live right here in Jershon forever. How about you?" She was now standing on the wooden bench, looking down on

Nathan, pretending to hold two babies one in each arm, laughing all the time.

All he could say was, "I only want eight."

Then she suddenly grew sullen. "I have nothing. My family has nothing. Our father died in the Lamanite army. We joined the people of God because we know that God loves us and his son Jesus Christ paid for our sins. We want to live with people that love God as we do. That's what I wish for Nathan. What do you want?"

"Dianna, when my father died, I was mad at God. I thought, how could he do this to me? I had to grow up. And thanks to my mother and sisters and grandfather, I grew to love work and service as I helped others. I know God lives and his son Jesus Christ will come to this earth and atone for our sins. I want to be an instrument in his hands to help other people, like my father and grandfathers."

They were now standing in the moonlight away from the rest of the friends. It was comfortable being with each other. Nathan slipped his hand to hold hers. Looking into her eyes, he said, "Will you walk with me in the night air?"

"Yes." She took his hand, and they strolled along, each deep in thought.

What was happening to them?

*****

Nathan managed the farm with mature wisdom beyond his years, which he attributed as a blessing from God, and he was thankful for that.

The harvest was completed for the year and stored away for the families. Much of it they would give to the Nephites to help maintain the armies to protect this land in which they lived. The harvest this year was better than most, an abundance of grain, vegetables preserved, and the herds expanding.

Nathan grew tall with lean muscles refined and hard from hours of work each day. He looked much like Ammon thirty years earlier, with broad shoulders and handsome features. Aaron was shorter by two inches, stocky and thick in his legs and midsection. Joel was more slight and slender, healthy but wiry. Each boy grew into a handsome young man. At eighteen, they each were wise beyond their years.

The three set off on a camping trip for a break from the labor of the season.

Joseph and Benjamin brought several young men from the farms to the west. Together at a favorite gathering place, a grand camping adventure began, which included swimming in the lake, fishing, and a rousing game of old sow. The fish were cleaned and stowed in a bag in the stream to keep the bears from smelling them. Anxious to get the game underway, everyone's attention turned to hole digging and fashioning sticks from nearby trees.

The game was on. Nathan was the old sow first. He moved the pig forward. Aaron jetted ahead, leaving his hole exposed. Swinging at the ball, Nathan checked the swing with his stick. A loud smack! As the sticks collided, the ball didn't move. Aaron pushed his backside against Nathan and pushed the ball with his stick. It rolled toward Joseph's hole. He bounded forward, leaving his hole unattended. Joel slipped into Joseph's hole, leaving Joseph in the middle with Aaron and Nathan. Three boys and two pockets. Each looked around, Nathan smacked the ball, sending it out of the circle and made a sprint for an open hole.

At the same time, Aaron and Joseph collided, shaking just a little, and dove for the extra pocket. Joseph's stick got there. First, he slid on one knee under Aaron's arm and said, "You're the old sow." Aaron ran, retrieved the pig, and the action began again. The longer the game went, the more aggressive the young men were, pushing shoving whacking, laughing, and moaning. They were enjoying exercise and friendship.

Many games ago, it was decided that if anyone got upset, they would sit out until they cooled down, then back they came ready to get hit.

The game went on for two hours. Sweaty and dusty, the boys called an end to the contest.

Everyone jumped back in the lake, washed, cooled down, and we're ready for dinner around the campfire. They settled into a camping place used several times over the years.

Covered with big pine trees and secluded, where the young men could have a fire, cook the fish caught in the nearby lake, and sit and discuss the problems of the world as they understood them.

Tonight several speckled large trout lay on the hot coals sizzling with crisp brown skin. Pots of corn and beans bubbled on the fire and flatbread browned on a rock. Joel seemed to be the best chef. Benjamin always helped. The others were okay with helping build a fire and clean up. Nathan produced a bag full of sweet cakes with berries and raisins. A gift from Dianna as he packed his bags that morning.

She said, "Here, Nathan, take these," and gave him a sweet innocent smile. "I thought you would enjoy them."

She was right. They were tasty after a supper of fish, corn, and beans with bread. The sweet cakes tasted delicious.

Aaron liked them especially and mentioned how nice it would be to have a sister to bake cakes for him.

Nathan only grunted and sighed, "Yeah."

For a long time, they just stared into the fire. Each captured by his thoughts.

Finally, Aaron said, "Would you fight if you needed to save our families?"

The question caught the others off guard. Each mulled the matter over for a moment. Then all tried to voice an opinion at once.

"Yes," squeaked Joel. "If it came to that, I would fight."

"Me too," chimed Nathan.

Joseph said, "I'll fight."

A voice from the crowd said, "What, their kneecaps?"

Joseph only smiled. "I'll fight."

Aaron continued, "Our fathers made a covenant never to take up arms to fight again."

"Right, right." Nathan, Joel, and the others agreed. "But we would stand in place for our fathers if it comes to that. Do you think it would be the right thing to do?"

Nathan took a deep breath and let it out with a sigh. "My father, as you know, gave his whole life to service for others after the covenant he made with God. It is my goal to stand as my father did and never take up arms toward anyone. But if it comes to that, I will take my stance with Captain Moroni and the Title of Liberty. Then I will pledge my life to protect my friends and my country." Nathan found himself standing, staring into the night, feeling somewhat silly. He was resolved to protect those he loved.

Aaron, Joel, Joseph, Benjamin, and every boy there stood with him, out in the wilderness next to their campfire, committing to fight. Little did these stripling warriors realize what was in store for them in the years to come.

# CHAPTER 14

## *A Time to Decide*

A message was sent out to each village, town, and farm in the land of Jershon, announcing a meeting to take place on the second day of next week. The message stated how vital it was for every family to attend. Of course, word traveled faster than the messenger's. Everyone was buzzing about Helaman coming to raise an army for the defense of the Nephite nation. It was widely known the war was not going well of all the Nephite cities captured or under siege by the Lamanites. The battles were coming. Several young men attending this meeting had visions of going off to slay the enemy.

The day of the meeting arrived, families came from every corner of the land. More than ten thousand strong showed up. The meeting place as always was referred to as the bowl because that's what it was. A hill rose on the west side, near a large grove of trees. Smaller hills formed a circle from west to north and east, leaving an opening to the south. Many years of exposure to water eroded the soil in benches from top to bottom after a few years. Grass grew over the entire bowl, making a perfect outdoor amphitheater. The audience could hear every word throughout the basin. As the people of Ammon settled Jershon, this became the central meeting place. All important meetings for the community began here.

Today the valley was full. The decisions today involved everyone. Neighbors sat with neighbors. Villagers sat together. Friends sat with friends, and families who hadn't seen each other for several months visited while the meeting got organized.

Ammon called the meeting to order and explained the need for an army to help Captain Moroni and the Nephites in the battle against the invading Lamanites. All in one motion, the men and fathers stood and said, "We will break the covenant we have made to protect our families and this country. We will go and fight for our brethren. They have been so kind to us. We feel the need to help them."

These were good men, honest, humble, changed by the light of Christ, from the life of Lamanites to men of God, with families. They started a new life in this new land, and they were ready to defend it with their lives if necessary.

Helaman stood. "My dear friends, I fear if you break this covenant, it will become a curse to you. I have an idea. Your sons did not make such a covenant. Will they come forward and fight for their country and families."

Most fathers protested. How could they stay home and let their sons fight in their place. At first, all wanted to break the covenant made years earlier—never to take up arms again to shed blood.

The fathers loved their sons. A surge of fear and sorrow went deep in each heart. How could they stand by and let the boys they loved go off to war. It was almost more than these fathers could bear, to have the young men fight, maybe die to protect the Nephites and the land of Jershon.

Only when Ammon and Helaman stood in the meeting and asked that the fathers stay home and the sons take up the sword to fight for this land did the people of Ammon agree.

So it was decided, the stripling warriors would carry the battle cry. They would raise the Title of Liberty. Now they needed a leader someone that would have the Spirit of God with him that would be fearless and yet humble.

Ammon spoke with authority. "My people you have made the right decision. Our young men will represent us well. We need a man of God to lead them."

Thousands of voices chanted, "Helaman, Helaman, Helaman. Lead us in defense of our country?"

Helaman bowed his head and said, "Indeed, I will."

People moved away in small groups, chatting quietly. Some spoke of the young age of the boys. Others asked, "Would God protect them?" Many of the mothers felt comfort from the Spirit that all would be right with their sons. All seemed at ease with Helaman as their leader.

Nathan's felt his heart would burst. He knew this was right. He would fight and die for his loved ones. Jumping to his feet, he shouted, "I will go." Aaron and Joel, standing beside him, linked arm in arm, feeling a little embarrassed.

People looked at these three boys standing in the half-empty amphitheater, shouting, "I will go." Soon others joined in, ready to commit to follow Helaman.

First, it was ten, then fifty, then a hundred came.

\*\*\*\*\*

From the road out past the stream, a rumbling sound of stomping feet, five hundred youth from the hill country with torches and songs of joy, marching songs. Five hundred from the villages along the river, tall kids, vigorous from pulling barges up and down the banks of the river. Farmers were coming in from the fields to the north, big husky boys that knew how to work. Several hundred showed up that day of the meeting and all wanting to take the place of their fathers. They were proud to stand in for their fathers as each one left his home. It became a sad farewell, young men going off to war armed with faith in Jesus Christ taught to them by their mothers, willing to give their lives for family, God, and country.

In the crowd from the hills were friends of Nathan, Aaron, Joel, and a strange pair—Joseph, the shortest stripling in the whole army, and Benjamin, one of tallest. The two boys were fast friends, having played old sow many hours with the other boys. Joseph was known as the ankle crusher and spared no one when in the heat of battle. Benjamin was known to throw down his stick and run for cover with Joseph hot on his tail swinging his stick after Benjamin's long, lean legs, forgetting all about the old sow ball.

Their families lived next to each other. They worked together, farmed together. Now, they were determined to fight. A few years before, while the two boys were floating out in the big lake near their farms, Joseph jumped off a handmade raft. While leaping for the water, his foot slipped on a wet log. He did a backflip, hitting his head on the wood, knocking him unconscious. Falling face down in the water, he began to go sink. Benjamin jumped in, reached his long arms around his small friend, and pushed him back upon the raft. After what seemed like an hour, which was only seconds, Joseph began breathing again, a significant bump raised on the back of his head. He was very dizzy for the rest of the day. Benjamin saved Joseph's life that day. Seldom did they speak about it, but a bond of love and friendship grew from the experience that made them inseparable. So they were there together, each ready to protect the other. Although many laughed at Little Joe, he would always say, "I have a guardian angel with me."

*****

Helaman divided the army into twenty groups of one hundred. Each group consisted of ten patrols with ten men. These patrols marched together, pitched tents together, ate together, and played old sow together, and looked out for each other.

Helaman stopped at Nathan's house and sat down with Sariah and her son.

"I want you to be my leader, to lead these stripling warriors, under my command. Can you do it?"

Nathan's mind raced for a moment. Could he serve as a leader and an example? He needed help.

"Yes," Nathan said, "I will do it if my grandfather will give me a blessing."

"That will be fine," replied Helaman.

The excitement of preparation was everywhere, Nathan, Aaron, and Joel made a pact to always stay together. Joseph and Benjamin insisted they be in the same patrol together. Most boys stayed with their friends and neighbors in the patrols.

The next few days were full. Supplies gathered and weapons secured, it would take a few months to get fully into the battle mode. This was the start. Eager with energy and enthusiasm, Helaman's army came together quickly. In two weeks, they were off to the front of the conflict.

Nathan received a blessing from his grandfather the last night they were home. The man of God gathered his family around, laid his hands on Nathan's head, and said, "In the name of the great Jehovah, I give you a blessing of protection, comfort, and peace, as you are obedient to the commandments of God. Help others be obedient to the teachings received from your mothers. Stay faithful. You will lead this army of God to perform miracles and receive protection to return to your loved ones. The story of your courage will inspire generations of young stripling warriors to fight for the army of God. In the name of the Eternal Father. Amen."

Tears flowed freely, and hugs lasted forever. Nathan stared out into the night and felt the presence of his father near.

Morning came quickly. Good-byes passed around to everyone.

Sariah said, "I love you, son. Take care."

"I will, Mom."

He hugged Dianna and ruffled her hair. "Take care of your mother."

Nathan kissed his sisters, and off he went a little scared.

Somewhat excited, filled with the spirit, knowing this was what God wanted these young men to do.

# CHAPTER 15

## *Becoming a Striping Warrior*

The word *stripling* means youth. Helaman's army comprised of young, handsome, full of strength, energy yet humble and teachable young men. They were full of faith and the desire to do what was right, ready to respond at the shout of a command from their leader. This willingness to act in a split second made them quick to strike. It would catch the enemy off guard. Many Lamanite paid the price of a swift stroke from the sword of a stripling warrior covering the back of the man next to him.

Two weeks of marching and Helaman's army arrived at the city Judea, under the command of General Antipus. These sons of Helaman were in great shape, having spent almost every day working in the fields. The mood in the camp was calm, confident, yet jovial and fun.

The first night in the city, Nathan called the young leaders of the army together. Questions came from every patrol. When do we fight, or will we be with the other Nephite troops? Is there a way to write home someday? They discussed the facts. Helaman would lead them into battle. Yes, they would fight with the other Nephite troops. As far as writing home, he would inquire when the opportunity came up. For now, the answer was, "We shall see." Also, was it permissible to play old sow? Yes, to old sow, just don't get to wild.

The meeting ended as Antipus and Helaman walked through the camp. The generals marveled at the order and spirit among the warriors. It was clean. The evening meal was in progress. Groups sat around eating and talking; others were sharpening weapons, repairing clothes. All seemed immersed in productive activities. There was a feeling that these young men were on the Lord's errand and they knew it.

Nathan, Aaron, and Joel sat with the others in the patrol. Joel cooked a dinner of bread and meat with a gravy, kind of pocket meat pie with dried fruit, peas, and water. It was easy to fix and easy to carry. They settled down as the two leaders came walking up. The boys shifted and stood. A game of old sow just started. The boys were about to join.

"Welcome to our camp, sir. How are you?"

Antipus took Nathan by the hand. "Is this the skinny little boy I met in Zarahemla a few years ago? Now look at you. A man, a big man. Nathan, you resemble your grandfather so much. He must be very proud of you."

"Thank you, sir."

"Sit," Helaman said. "Are my sons ready?" He asked a question he already knew the answer.

"Yes," was the reply from all the boys at the same time. "We are ready."

"What's this game you're always playing?"

"Well, sir, my grandfather taught it to us several years ago. It's the game all of Jershon wants to play."

"I see, something like battle training."

"Yes, it can get rough. For the most part, we keep it friendly."

Helaman looked a bit puzzled. "With clubs, holes in the ground, everyone running around swinging their sticks at that ball, it seems fun but dangerous."

"Would you like to join in?" Nathan asked.

"Not tonight. We want to start a plan tomorrow to help build the defenses around the city and practice Warfare. Here is a schedule for each leader. We will begin working on the west wall, with afternoon drilling in the central courtyard."

"This is a good plan. We will fortify this city and be prepared to go against the Laminates."

*****

Antipus looked on in amazement, watching the stripling warriors work on the wall. These young men were strong and happy. Moving piles of dirt and rocks seemed to be no challenge to them. Nathan organized groups of tens making progress on the wall roll smooth and steady. Everyone knew his job and his responsibility.

Day after day, the walls increased in height. After the rocks, dirt. Then timbers and pickets placed on top made these walls impenetrable. Easy to defend against an enemy.

It took the next few months to build up the defenses. Practicing warfare became a daily exercise.

After the first session of drills, Nathan, Aaron, Joel, Joseph, and Benjamin sat, eating the evening meal.

Nathan spoke. "What we need is a way to signal to every warrior in a minute's notice when to move, to advance, or to spin left or right, when to shoot his bow or use his sword. What do you think?"

Aaron proclaimed, "I know how we can do it! Who has the loudest voice here? Joseph?"

"Yes," everyone agreed.

"We will have Joseph be our flag bearer, shouting one-word commands."

"Yes, yes," shouted Benjamin. "I would stand next to Joseph and be his guard."

Nathan again spoke up. "We need four or five maneuvers. If we move in a fluid motion all at the same time, we can become like one body, something the Lamanites have never witnessed before."

"That sounds good," stated Joel."

"Our first maneuver should be the flying *V*. You know when geese fly in a *V*, drafting off the goose in front of them. We can cover each other in a flying wedge. Five hundred broad two deep, guarding each other a line on the left, a line on the right spread in a *V* formation. Joseph will shout a command he receives from Helaman, 'Wedge.' He then will hold a yellow banner. All will know this is for the flying wedge and instantly move into formation. Bows and arrows ready, moving in unison against the enemy. Shoot, step back. The next line steps forward, fires, steps back. The first group steps forward, aims, fires again. The shooting continuing until Helaman gives another command."

"The next movement should be swords," stated Aaron. "As we get into closer range, swords came out. Shields made ready. We move into two $U$ shapes with Helaman in the center as he gives the command. Joseph holds up a green banner shaped in a $U$ and shouts, 'Swords.' Instantly, the warriors move into $U$ formation with swords and shields ready to engage the enemy."

"Now we need to advance in a rapid movement," shouts Benjamin, getting caught up in the excitement of planning the attack movements. "We could call it the old sow movement. Move in with swords and clubs low and wild, swinging for legs and arms or any body part that gets in the path of the club."

"That does have some good points," Nathan said.

"If we stay close together and move fast, it keeps the Lamanites off guard. A red banner with a pig means to advance, the command from Helaman. Joseph will shout, 'Forward.'"

"Number four will be circle," Nathan stated. "We will use two forms an outside circle and an inside circle. Meaning the enemy will be on the inside circle or outside the circle. Each warrior will stand one foot apart, weapons ready, making ready for the enemy to surrender or fight the outside ring. A blue ring for this banner, and the command 'Circle outside, circle inside' from Helaman. Joseph will shout, 'Inside circle or outside.' Do you think it will work?"

By this time, a dozen or more young men were standing listening to the suggestions. All agreed. It will work.

*****

The next morning Nathan, Aaron, and Joel laid the plan out for Anitpus and Helaman. Both men were impressed. The idea became the practice drills each day until they moved and flowed as a whole body. Smooth and precise, following every command. Joseph made the banners so he could switch the colors instantly, then mounted them on a long pole fixed tall red feathers on his helmet. Being the shortest warrior, he was tough from living on his farm.

As the army marched in practice, the banners could be seen high above the warriors and a bunch of red feathers bouncing along and a booming voice shouting, "Circle, forward, wedge, or swords—Helman leading." The body of these stripling warriors was moving in a smooth motion.

With Nathan on the right and Benjamin on the left, Helaman would be in the middle. Aaron and Joel were behind Nathan. They practiced every day. After a long day of work and practice drills, dinner and a time to study followed by a game of old sow and then off to bed to start over again the next day.

As the year came to an end, a mailbag was gathered and heading to Zerahamla stopping in Jershon. There wasn't much time to write a long letter, so Nathan wrote a few lines.

Dear Mother,

I am doing good. We work hard and practice warfare every day. How is everything at home? I miss you all. Is the farm doing all right? Tell the girls I love them and miss them.

Mom, thanks for teaching me to have faith and to believe in Christ, I know we will be protected. Tell Grandpa hello and that I love him also. You're the best mother a stripling warrior could have. I love you. Please take care.

Love,
Nathan

As the new year began, the stripling warriors were ready to take the fight to the Lamanites. And so it began. A miracle would follow these young warriors, a blessing pronounced almost five hundred years before by Father Lehi. A blessing of protection for the righteous descendants of Laman.

Solemnly each warrior retired to his bed, knowing on the morrow, the battle would come at last.

# CHAPTER 16

## *Battle with the Lamanites*

Nathan's legs were shaking, his mouth was dry, and his voiced cracked as he shouted to his cousins, "Pray for God's protection."

"I am, I am," cried Aaron.

Joel, his other cousin, stood silent. He began to hum a song from their childhood.

The Lamanites came in waves, heads shaved, grotesque images painted on their torso, wearing only an animal skin dipped in blood around their loins and sandals to protect their feet. Their faces were dark and evil. Yellow teeth gnashing, they came close.

Nathan could smell their sweat and body scent. He could hear the chants and howling a sound that made him shudder.

The stripling warriors were well protected. Each had a helmet covering their head. They had a tunic with sleeves of leather covering their body with a breastplate strapped over the tunic, protecting their head and upper body. Each warrior wore a pair of short-legged pants fitted around the waist, the legs of the pants reaching just below the knees. The front was covered with thick leather and fabric sewn under the leather. Knee-high sandal boots covered the feet and lower legs After a few days, the shoes form-fitted each foot and were comfortable to march in.

There was a variety of weapons issued to the young men. Each carried a bow and quiver full of arrows, a sword molded after the Sword of Laban, and a short club with sharp rocks embedded in the head of the club that was very useful in close combat. They had a knife at their waist with a round shield attached to their left arm by leather straps. A leather bag hung at their side carrying some bandages, food, water, a few other odds and ends that each young man wanted.

Antipus, the general over the army, planned well. So far, it had worked. The stripling warriors marched out, drawing the Lamanites after them for three days. What a smart plan. Now the Lamanites stopped chasing the stripling warriors and turned on Antipus's army, who was behind the Lamanites. It was now time to turn and march into the fight.

Helaman called them together and spoke. "Are you ready to fight?"

"Yes," they shouted. "Let us protect our families and loved ones."

"Let us kneel in prayer." Helaman offered a short but powerful prayer. "Father, we offer our strength and honor, our faith, and, if necessary, our lives to protect our freedom and our families. Help us to obey and listen to thy Spirit and be an instrument in thy hands today, Amen." Then Helaman shouted, "Make ready your weapons. Obey my commands, and you shall live to see your families again."

Joseph raised the red pig banner and shouted, "Advance."

With that, the army started at a fast trot.

Helaman drew the Sword of Laban. It glistened in the morning sun. Nathan could feel the power of the sword, and all fear dissipated like fog in the daybreak.

Power and strength entered each heart of the stripling warriors as they fell on the rear flank of the whole Lamanite army.

"Form a wedge," ordered Helaman.

Joseph shoved the yellow banner into the air and cried, "Wedge."

Instantly, a flying wedge-formed.

Helaman at the point, every young warrior following his every command.

Helaman would command in a loud voice, "*Bow*."

Joseph shouted, "*Bow*," waving the yellow banner.

A volley of arrows flew with deadly accuracy.

Again and again the order, "Bow," and a barrage rained down on the unprotected Lamanites, bringing death with every step.

Beginning to retreat, the Lamanites gave way to the deadly arrows of the warriors, scattering to get out of range, firing back sporadically at the striplings, occasionally hitting one in the leg or arm, which caused some bleeding. But after a quick bandage wrap, most were up and back into the fight, pressing forward.

Helaman cried, "Swords."

Joseph screamed, "Swords" and thrust the green banner skyward.

The troops moved into a *U* shape, just like they practiced a thousand times, swords drawn and shields ready. The Sword of Laban was swinging and striking with every stroke. The stripling warriors were moving forward. The warriors cut through the Lamanite army, reaching the army of Anitpus. He lay dead, killed by the Lamanites.

Nathan stopped for a moment and thanked God for such a brave man to give his life for his country. The battle must go on, so all Nathan could do was rally the troops to get them to gain there fortitude. The Nephite army was in disarray.

Suddenly Helaman shouted, "Wedge."

Joseph echoed, "Wedge." Instantly, a yellow banner flew above the battle.

The army of Antipus marveled at the skill and courage of these boys. In all their battles, never had they seen such a fighting force.

These young Ammonites were pushing through the Lamanites. A rallying cry went up. The wedge of Ammonites was very deadly. One thousand stripling warriors on each wing sweeping through the center of the enemy. Helaman, near the point of the wedge, shouted orders and commands to his young sons.

Helaman would command in a loud voice, "*Bow*," and a short comical warrior with large red feathers in his helmet would shout Helaman's every command. A volley of arrows flew with deadly accuracy. Again, he would order, "Bow," and a second volley rained down on the unprotected Lamanites. "Sword forward," and the Ammonites followed Helaman's every command. The Sword of Laban shone brightly in the morning sun. A U-shaped formation formed quickly, swords and shields cutting through the unprotected lines of Lamanites. They were back peddling to escape the oncoming Ammonites.

The red pig banner went up. "Forward," came the command, and on they came, overrunning the most powerful army of the Lamanites. Fear showed in their eyes. Who were these warriors with such power, so well trained? Some unseen force protected them. The Lamanites turned to run. When the command came, "Circle inside," a blue banner raised slowly over the field of battle. With a swift motion, a circle formed. The army of the Lamanites found themselves surrounded, being cut off from escape.

"Surrender or die," Helaman shouted.

Most Lamanites could see the battle was over. Captured in a circle, every stripling warrior held a bow or a sword pointed at the captives.

"Cast down your weapons and kneel on the ground."

A few resisted at first. At the point of a sharp sword, Lamanites discarded their weapons in an enormous pile and kneeled on the ground. The battle was over, victory achieved. The enemy huddled together, looking for a chance to escape.

Helaman strode through his army of stripling warriors searching for those injured or killed. Helaman gave orders to his leaders to gather the dead and give them a decent resting place, feeling of foreboding sorrow hung over like a cloud. The soldiers of Antipus suffered a significant loss. Many a good man lay dead on the battlefield, and several hundred had wounds that required attention. Helaman rushed toward his young Ammonites, where they were gathering. His mind raced through the last three hours. The stripling warriors were incredible, mighty, so obedient to his commands, so brave in the face of overwhelming odds, yet never faltering, never backing down, just moving forward with the Spirit of God in their hearts and minds. In all his life, Helaman never witnessed a more fearless and ferocious group of warriors. But how many were lost? His heart was heavy as he approached their camp.

Nathan was the first to greet him with a white bandage wrapped around his left forearm and a gash of about an inch long under his chin, which left a neat-looking scar he would wear the rest of his life as a badge of honor.

"How many are lost?" were the first words out of Helaman's mouth.

Nathan was kneeling next to Joel. Bloodstains were on Joel's left leg. There was a wide gash across his leg bandaged with a green paste slathered over the cut. A white bandage bound the wound.

Nathan stood, with tears in his eyes he turned to Helaman and spoke in a humble tone. "All were wounded, but none were lost. We are all alive."

Helaman took a deep breath and replied, "Let us kneel and thank our God for such a blessing."

This time Nathan said the short but powerful prayer. "Father, we thank thee for preserving our lives and blessing us with the strength and power for this victory, Amen."

There were two thousand echoes. "Amen."

Aaron turned and asked Nathan, "Will you give me some of that green paste?"

"Yes, it's in that jar." Handing him a red clay pot.

"What's this stuff?" their general asked.

"It's a paste my mother makes for all the injuries we had growing up. She mixes plants and roots. It stinks and is very painful to apply, but most wounds heal in two days. We call it Sariah Salve."

"I see we have more miracles than one here today."

"Yes, we do."

Gathering up the warriors, they started back to the city of Judea, helping those that were wounded. Most of the wounds came from the close hand-to-hand fighting. There were cuts on hands and legs, and one young man had an arrow in his foot. After stepping on the shaft, the point rammed through his foot. With some green salve, a lot of screaming, and some teasing, he healed fine. The stripling warriors recovered amazingly fast.

*****

Helaman came to Nathan in his weekly meeting of all the patrol leaders.

Drawing a makeshift map, he said, "Word came to us. A Lamanite supply army is passing near the west hills between us and the northern cities. If we can surprise the train and capture the provisions, it will deal a severe blow to the Lamanites who are low on food and supplies. We plan to leave tonight after dark, travel silent up the north side of the creek when the stream turns toward the lake. There is a lot of brush and small scrub trees alongside the banks of the stream. It's a full moon tonight. I feel the Lamanites well try to sneak by us, moving at night. We will attack them from a hiding place in the brush and capture the provisions and return to Judea by sunrise. Make ready to leave as soon as the sun goes down."

"Yes, sir."

The army moved out in silence, staying undercover as much as possible, marching forward at a breakneck pace.

They reached the area in two hours, setting the warriors on both sides of the road hidden in the brush. They waited for about three hours. The sound of men and horses moving along the path came crisp in the night air. All made ready as the train passed by. The Lamanites seemed tired and worn-out at the command of Helaman and the echo of Joseph, "Circle," screamed through the valley.

Two thousand stripling warriors sprang out of the brush, a blue banner thrust into the air. Catching the Lamanites off guard, the warriors rushed forward. The Ammonites formed a complete circle with swords and shields at the ready.

The fighting commenced. Lamanites tried to run, only to find no place to escape. They then tried to fight but were cut down as the Ammonites' advance brought death with every blow.

Some Lamanites hid under the provisions but to no advantage. They were surrounded. Three hundred died at the first onslaught. Realizing to fight was useless, the Lamanites called, "Quarter," and knelt on the ground.

Helaman shouted, "Throw down your weapons."

Joseph echoed, "Throw down your weapons."

Swords lay on the grass, then on a command from the Lamanite leader, two hundred jumped and rushed straight into the line of warriors, meeting sharp swords. Much clamor and confusion followed. The Lamanite leader slammed into Benjamin, knocking him off his feet and also rolling Joseph over. Into the brush went six Lamanites.

Benjamin rolled and jumped to his feet and was after the escapees, with Joseph three steps behind, as they cleared the brushy cover of the stream in the moonlight.

The running Lamanites labored up a steep incline.

Benjamin stopped and drew his bow. "Twang, twang," sounded Joseph's bow a second later. Two runners slumped and died.

As the Lamanites reached the hilltop, *thud-thud*, two more paid the price of stopping for one second too long.

Benjamin sprinted forward. His long legs galloping up the hill. Behind him Little Joe's shorter legs were pumping faster but not covering as much ground. The chief of the Lamanites stopped and gave his companion in front of him a shove and scrambled under an enormous pine tree, burying himself with pine needles.

The lone Lamanite stood caught as Benjamin sprinted forward and raised his sword to deliver a death blow. The chief stabbed Benjamin in the belly with his sword. *Twang*, a bowstring sounded from behind him. Joseph ended the lone Lamanite's life.

The chief Lamanite rushed forward, pulling his sword from Benjamin's belly as Ben toppled over to the ground and curled into a ball.

Joseph went to his old sow stance, sword low and swinging, shield protecting his head and shoulders. The chief marveled at this small warrior, how easy it would be to kill him. He rushed forward. The leader had never played old sow with Joseph. With his sword high above his head, the Lamanite moved in for the kill, only to feel a sharp pain in his right knee as it buckled. He slammed to the ground writhing in shock.

Screaming, he jumped up, swinging wildly at this mini warrior, never hitting his mark. Coming so close, Joseph could smell his stench. Then his patterned old sow move kicked in, step forward and trust, his sword found the target. The chief's eyes rolled back in his head. His wounded big body, no longer able to stand, fell forward, smashing into Joseph, knocking both to the ground.

Little Joe lay pinned under a two-hundred-pound dead Lamanite. All the air rushed out of his lungs. He gasped for breath and caught the foul smell from this body. He grunted and groaned, pushed wiggled, and finally squeezed out from under the dead weight.

Jumping to his feet, Joseph rushed to Benjamin's side. The bleeding stopped. His eyes fluttered open, "I am hurt, Joe, real bad."

"Hang on, and I'll get you out of here and back to camp." Joseph worked fast. He dug into his bag. Grabbed some Sariah Salve, and a bandage. He cleaned the wound and applied a generous amount of the salve, which caused Benjamin to grimace some. Then he bandaged his best friend's belly.

Kneeling, Joseph offered a pleading prayer. "Dear Father in heaven, my best friend is hurt bad. I need your help to get him back to camp. I know you can do all things. Please give me the strength to pull him now. I love you and your Son, Amen. Oh, this is Joseph."

Next, he took Ben's shield, tying two leather straps to it, one on each side. Making a harness to pull the sleigh with his shoulders, he packed his weapons and tied Benjamin on the shield. Then he was off through the brush, over the rocks, trying to find the road where the battle took place, hoping to find some help.

*****

At the battle scene, two hundred Lamanite prisoners tried to escape, running straight into the warriors, meeting sharp swords and death, until they realized escape was futile and again knelt in submission. Only six prisoners broke through. In the confusion, only Benjamin and Joseph noticed and gave chase. Nathan gathered the prisoners, tied them together, and marched back to the city of Judia.

As the sun rose in the east, all patrol leaders reported in a few wounds and all accounted for except one patrol reported Joseph and Benjamin missing.

Nathan's heart sunk. He could not remember when he last saw the two friends. The escape attempt drew attention in several directions at one time, and no one remembered seeing Ben and Joe leave the circle. Nathan called the warriors together and told them Ben and Joe were missing. The whole company wanted to go after them even though being up all night.

Helaman said, "Nathan, Aaron, and Joel will go find them. They can travel fast and silent. There are bands of Lamanites roaming around trying to find any unsuspecting Nephite. If they do, they will rob and kill them. Go quickly, find our brothers, and bring them home." Helaman handed Nathan the Sword of Laban and said, "Take this, son. God will protect you."

Slipping out the side gate, they moved into the cover of the trees, staying away from the roads, heading back to the battleground.

After two hours, Nathan slowed to a walk and moved toward the trail. In the distance, a lone figure small and mighty struggled, pulling something slowly behind him. The three Ammonites burst into a full gallop as they recognized Joseph struggling with a burden pulling behind him.

Suddenly, out of the brush jumped a swarm of Lamanites at least ten in the bunch. Swords raised, coming full speed, bent on killing Joseph.

Before the warriors could reach him, Nathan stopped, reached in his bag, pulled out his sling, and a hand full of smooth stones. The first Lamanites were closing in on Joseph, his short legs pumping fast but going slower and slower.

Nathan let the first stone fly. *Twack*. Down toppled the closest enemy. *Whap*. Down went another. The rest of the Lamanite stopped in their tracks. *Thud*, right between the eyes. Nathan's aim was uncanny. He could hit a bird in flight back home with his sling when out hunting.

Aaron and Joel doubled their pace, reaching Joseph ahead of Nathan. Looking down at Benjamin strapped to his shield, awake but woozy, Joseph shouted, "Am I happy to see you."

Joel looked at him. "Joseph, how did you pull this all the way?"

Joseph said, "He's not heavy. He's my brother. Let's get out of here."

With one warrior on each side, they flew down the road past Nathan. Seven Lamanites strung out, facing this stripling warrior, who resembled his grandfather at the waters of Sebus. The Sword of Laban shone in the morning sun. God protects the man that carried this sword. Nathan leaped into the roadway, sword high above his head, now striking swiftly like a snake, severing body parts with each motion.

His fluid movement confused the Lamanites. As this warrior ended the attack, seven bodies lay strewn over the road. It was over. His friends were save. He sheathed the sword and trotted after the others, back to the city to get some rest and maybe a game of old sow.

\*\*\*\*\*

This army grew in stature and wisdom. A few months later, sixty more stripling warriors joined them. Provisions from the people of Ammon came and letters from home. Nathan helped pass out all the letters each family sent. It was quiet around the camp that night. Everyone sat and read the messages from home, then reread them. Most wrote letters to send back as a garrison heading to Zarahelema was scheduled at sunrise the next morning with the mailbag.

Nathan opened his letter.

Dear Nathan,

We received your letter last year as the company passed through Jershon. We received word two weeks ago to have a message ready, so the whole family sat as I wrote this letter. Everyone is doing great here. Naomi and Dianna took over most of the farming. Ruth and Sara care for the garden and animals. Asher helps everyone. Asa still tries to do the housework, but she has poor health some days. I am overseeing the whole place. We do miss you so much. The word from the war is it is going well, and you may be coming home in a year or two. I hope that is true, son. The cows give Naomi and Dianna fits each summer, trying to keep them in the pasture. Both girls work hard to maintain the fences and fields. God blesses us every year with a bountiful harvest. We give thanks for your safety and hope this letter finds you full of joy. All the girls send their love. Grandfather is away helping other people get settled. He also sends his love. Nathan, we pray for you each night and look for the day when you will return home to us.

Love,
Your family

A lump came to his throat, how he longed for home, to sit on the back step at night and watch the sunset over the fields and listen to the night sounds come alive in the stream and ponds—frogs, birds, crickets. He missed the smell of supper cooking in the kitchen and the sound of chatter from the girls over silly things, and he missed Dianna. He wondered if he would ever have a son go off to fight for his country.

He thought, *I need to scribble a note to my family.*

Dear Mother,

I just got your letter. Thank you for sending it. I miss you and the whole family. Life here is tough. We have been in many battles.

I have observed many miracles. Remember Little Joe and Benjamin? They had a close scrap a few months back. Benjamin got wounded. He has recovered now thanks to the Sariah Salve, or that's what we call the green stuff. We use if after every battle. Mom, God has protected us, everyone. The army of Helaman has all received wounds. No one has died while thousands of the Nephite soldiers die.

We look forward to the day when this conflict is over, and we can return to our homes.

Until then, we will stand with Captain Mornori and the Title of Liberty.

Helaman leads us to victory, and God protects us. How can we fail? We have faith because our mothers taught us to believe in the teachings of Christ, and we all have faith in his miraculous power. Thanks, Mom, for teaching me.

Tell all the family I love them.

I will be home someday.

Love,
Nathan

*****

Out on a march one night, Helaman discovered an army of five thousand Lamanites sneaking through a forest to come behind the city of Cumeni from the backside.

The Lamanites camped just inside, a forest of towering pine trees with huge branches high off the ground. The forest stretched for about five miles, the main road cutting through the center with high hills on each side, a perfect hiding place for an army to sneak around the city of Cumeni and attack from the back.

Dividing his forces, Helaman secreted around the camp of the Lamanites and marched on for two miles. Two thousand warriors climbed into the trees; the other sixty covered all the tracks and marched a short distance.

There they made a makeshift camp, with fires, tents, and soldiers walking around. Creating the appearance of a busy camp making ready for sleeping, guards set up to make the Lamanites think this camp was guarding the back entrance to the city.

Meanwhile, Helaman sent runners to the city to bring more soldiers. An army of one thousand came back and hid in the trees and rocks. The Lamanite army was up and marching before sunup. They saw the camp of the stripling warriors. Wanting to surprise them, they rushed forward through the trees on the road, hoping to catch the Ammonites sleeping. As they sped past the stripling warriors hiding in the trees, not one Lamanite looked up. The stripling warriors sat perfectly still as the Lamanites rushed through the trees, so anxious to deal a death blow to these Ammonites. Oh, how little they knew the power of the Spirit that attended the stripling warriors. On his command, two thousand tree-dwellers dropped behind the Lamanite army.

Nathan shouted the command, "Wedge," and Joseph repeated, "Wedge." A yellow banner flew in the early morning air. At the same time, Helaman, commanding the army in front, shouted, "Wedge." A yellow flag rose from that end of the battle. The flying wedge formed instantly behind and in front bow. A volley of arrows flew among the surrounded Lamanites caught in a barrage of shooting warriors. The second volley of arrows found many a target. Bodies dropped everywhere. The Lamanite moved closer into a circle for protection, tripping over bodies and stumbling to get in a fighting stance. Bow again. The unrelenting rain of arrows came down on the Lamanites. Finally, grabbing their swords, the Lamanite mounted a charge at the front army.

Just as the command came, "Swords," bellowed over the ruckus, a green banner floated in the morning breeze. Then shields and swords came up, slashing forward, moving the back closer to the front with each step, closing in for the final blow.

"Forward," shouted both leaders, and the red pig struck the air. With a double-time pace, the stripling warriors moved in, causing the Lamanites to turn and run, only to meet the sharp point of a sword the other direction. Soon it was clear the Lamanites were defeated. The circle in command floated over the battle with a blue banner. The Lamanites knelt.

"Face down" came the order.

Helaman was taking no chance of a breakout from the prisoners. The weapons secured and prisoners tied together, they marched into the city to build and secure the walls.

These young soldiers became a fighting force known for having such power and courage. Their acclaim grew as they fought to free the Nephite nation. Many battles won by these sons of Helaman showed how miraculous was their faith and obedience to Helaman's commands.

*****

Around the fire one night after a hard-fought battle, men came by to use some of the green paste, so popular among the troops after each battle. It seemed almost to have a power of healing like nothing ever witnessed before.

They sat by the fire and asked, "Why did you come to the war? And how is it none of you ever perish while thousands of our soldiers die?"

Nathan spoke up. "We believe in the lessons taught to us by our mothers. If we have faith in Jesus Christ, we are promised protection. We are obedient to Helaman's orders, and the Spirit of God leads him in the fights. We pray a lot. That sustains each of us moment by moment in the heat of battle. After, we always give thanks for being preserved and protected. That, sir, is what keeps us going."

*****

Years passed, many longed for this war to be over and wished to be back with their families, but they were firm and faithful to the end.

The Lamanites, determined to make one last stand to drive out the Nephites, gathered a large army and captured many cities. The Nephite army pulled back to maintain the land they held. A battle commenced as the Lamanites attacked a supply army of the Nephites on the way to bring provisions to the command of Helaman. At this time, the stripling warriors were out on patrol.

Having marched three days without rest, word came to Helaman, a battle was in progress and the Lamanites were attacking a supply train of provisions meant for the Ammonites. Helaman gathered his leaders and gave them the grim news. Ten miles away the Lamanites were engaging a Nephite army and stealing supplies meant for them. Could they get there in time to save the army? The only answer was, "*Yes,*" and off they went.

They covered ten miles in two hours. Coming over a slight hill, the Nephites were in a circle with the wagons of the supplies, fighting for their lives, suffering heavy losses. The remainder of the soldiers were ready to surrender to save more loss of life. Just as the Ammonites stopped on the hilltop, they raised the red banner, the *pig.* Shields and swords came out. A mighty shout came from the trapped Nephites, "*We are saved. Praise God.*"

The battle stopped, and the Lamanites turned to see the army they feared the most marching in double-time straight at them. The red banner flowing in the breeze and that sword shining in the sunshine, Heleman's army came like a tidal wave.

Helaman was leading the charge. At his sides stood a group of fierce warriors on his command. A flying wedge formed. A short stripling with tall red feathers in his helmet screamed, "Bow."

The Lamanites tried to form a line to face the stripling warriors. Then the dreaded command came, heard so many times before by these Lamanites.

"*Bow.*"

And it started the rain of arrows. What just a few minutes ago was a sure victory and needed provisions, now became a disaster and no place to retreat.

On they came again, bow and that sword. Forward they came.

The Lamanites, soon in full panic, ran for the trees only to be met by the Nephites.

"Circle," came the cry, and a short warrior with red feathers in his headgear shouted, "Circle," and a blue banner flew In the afternoon sky, swords and shields went out and the battle got into close quarters. These warriors seem fearless, strong, and agile, covering each other's back.

The Lamanites were determined to fight to the death. They were surrounded. The battle continued.

Finally, with fewer than a thousand left alive, the Lamanites laid down their weapons and kneeled on the ground.

The battle ended. All prisoners were tied together and marched back to the city.

The stripling warriors escorted the Nephite army.

\*\*\*\*\*

Finally, the day came when all was secure in the land.

One night, Helaman came by the camp where Nathan, Joel, and Aaron were staying. He said, "I would like to speak to all 2,060 of you tomorrow night. Meet me near this small hill. I have news for you. We shall have a feast and a Council."

The following evening at sundown, a great feast was prepared for the stripling warriors by citizens from the nearby city. The roast lamb, bread, fruit, plates of vegetables, sweet cakes—everything was delicious.

After the meal, Helaman arose. His eyes were moist.

"My young friends, over these past years, I have come to love you as my sons. You are the greatest fighting force the Nephite nation has ever witnessed. Thank you for your courage, your obedience, your faith, and your skills. You have preserved our freedom. I know all of you were wounded, but none were lost because of the blessing and power of God. My young friends, many generations from now, your story will be told in a book prepared by the hand of God, our Father. It will inspire many people to live as you have lived and to center their lives on Jesus Christ as you have. In life, we are all wounded. Because of the Savior, none are lost. I love each of you. May God bless you. How would you like to go home starting tomorrow?"

A mighty shout erupted, "God bless Helaman. Praise God for our dear leader."

A flood of feelings came over 2,060 sons of Helaman. They felt joy, happiness, and gratitude, shouting in unison, "Yes, we are ready to go home."

# CHAPTER 17

## *Coming Home*

Nathan stretched out on his bed, which was a thick wool blanket covering a sheepskin. It was comfortable. He always slept sound after a long day of work or fighting. His wounds healed fast, and the scars were fading away. He felt an overflowing of gratitude tonight for all the tender mercies his Father in heaven showered down on him and his fellow stripling warriors.

It was such a long time this war carried on. Now it was over. God blessed the Nephites with a victory. The cost of this war in human lives was tremendous; almost every family was affected. Many lost fathers, brothers, sons—such a high price to pay for freedom. How thankful he was for leaders like Helaman, Captain Moroni, Teancum, Antipus, and Pahoran. What great vision they had, willing to give all they possessed, even their lives, to secure freedom for the nation. As Nathan drifted off to sleep, he thought of home and his family. Oh, how he missed his sisters, his mother, his grandfather, and Dianna. That was strange to him. He hadn't thought of her in months. Nathan remembered how cute she was and how enjoyable life was working alongside her in the fields and teasing her, splashing water in her face at the well. Tonight, in a very long time, he thought, *I hope she still lives at our home with us.* And the thought worried him. She might be married or moved to another area in Jershon or have a boyfriend. Silently, his thoughts came, *I wish I had treated her better.*

Then the little voice in his head said, "Well, you did treat her pretty good."

"Yes," he sighed. "It will be nice to see her."

He drifted off to sleep as his thoughts turned to Heth, back to the days of working alongside his father. The outings in the forest, sleeping under the stars, listening to stories from the brass plates. He wished for that time again as sleep overcame his mind. He looked in the distance and saw a figure tall and white walking toward him. Nathan peered as he recognized the personage. It was his father. There seemed to be a barrier between them. They could communicate through thoughts.

His father said how proud he was of Nathan and what a fine young man he was. Nathan told his father how much he loved and missed him.

Heth asked, "Will you take care of our family until we all meet again."

Nathan said he would. The last words communicated were, "Stay true to those things you believe in and have fought to maintain." Then the image was gone.

It seemed Nathan lay in his bed several hours, pondering the dream he just experienced.

As the sun rose, he stirred and got up. He felt refreshed, ready to journey home.

Joel was packing his pack. He yawned and said, "What will it be like to be home? What will we do? I suppose we'll go on with life. See what God has in store for us next. I do know one thing. I want to live next to you and Aaron and let my kids play with yours and tell stories of our adventures in the army of Helaman."

"Sounds magnificent to me. Let's get going!"

They fell into formation with their patrol, Helaman leading the way. Off they went at a brisk pace with Jershon on each young mind.

It took two weeks to cover the trail. It was a pleasant hike. Joy filled the hearts of the young Ammonites.

*****

Sariah felt down in the dumps, not just for one reason. She missed her husband, and she yearned for her son, Nathan, who was off fighting with Helaman. She wondered when this war would be over.

And as only a mother can, she longed to have her family around her tonight. They were growing fast. Naomi and Dianna were growing into beautiful young ladies, and Ruth was a fair young thing also. Tonight Sariah felt older than usual as she sat on the back porch preparing corn and potatoes for a stew. Dinner would be later tonight. It was spring. A new calf came to the old milk cow today.

Dianna and Naomi stayed out at the barn caring for the new calf, seeing she got dried off and was feeding on her mother. Aza, Dianna's mother, just finished the washing for the week. She gathered the clothes off the lines out back, folded them, and put away everyone's clothes in each room. Sariah sighed. Life was enjoyable for her family. Tomorrow, she would feel better. Tonight she would reread Nathan's last letter, received in the fall. That would help.

Sariah stood with her back to the doorway. A strange feeling came over her like someone was watching her. She knew she was all alone in the kitchen. The hair on her neck prickled. Out of the side vision of her eye, she saw motion. Spinning around, her mouth gaped wide open. A scream started, but no sound came. Her heart went a hundred beats a minute. Sariah dropped the bowl that was in her hands. Her mind raced to a thousand thoughts. A Lamanite warrior was standing in her doorway in full battle gear. Her first thought was to grab the broom for protection. Then her heart melted as she heard the words, "Mother, I am home." Dropping the broom, she flew across the floor, not even noticing the broken bowl and did a flying leap into the arms of the stripling warrior. "Oh, Nathan, Nathan. I love you." And they held each other tight for several moments, tears of joy streaming down their faces.

At last, Sariah pulled Nathan over to the table and sat him down. "Tell me what's happening."

Nathan said, "Well, I guess I will stay for dinner."

Sariah said, "You will stay forever. Nathan, how was the war?"

"Mom, it is the worst experience in this world. I have seen things I hope I never have to experience again. I also know that God is in our lives every day. He loves and blesses us with all we have. I know his Son, Jesus Christ, will come into this world to save us from our sins, and he loves the Lamanites as much as he does the Nephites. I am thankful to share a brotherhood with the army of Helaman. It was a privilege to serve my country, my family, and my God."

Ruth and Sara walked in with Asher, who screamed at the sight of a warrior sitting with Sariah. Suddenly recognizing Nathan, they pounced in his lap. They covered him in hugs and kisses, shouting, "He's home! He's home!"

Asa looked in to see what all the noise was. She skipped over and gave Nathan a huge hug. "Welcome home."

Naomi came bounding into the room. What a commotion, squealing, crying, laughing, hugs, kisses.

After about a half hour, Ammon walked in. He was bent a little, with pure white hair, looking like an angel. Nathan gave him a firm hug, and tears ran down both faces. All they could say was, "Thanks be to our God."

Sariah excused herself for a moment and said, "Dinner is almost ready. Let's sit down. I'll be right back."

The family took their familiar places at the table. Everyone sat quietly, smiling happily.

Sariah came in and asked, "Dad, will you sit at that end of the table and Nathan can sit at this end."

Next to Nathan was an empty chair. He looked around. Who was missing? A strange feeling came into Nathan's heart. He was talking to his mother and Ammon when someone entered the room. Turning, he looked. There in the doorway stood the most beautiful girl Nathan had ever seen. Her auburn hair flowed over her shoulders, freckles dotted a beautiful tanned smiling face. Large brown eyes gazed over the table, then rested on the empty chair next to Nathan.

He stood. A broad smile beamed across his face as he said, "You are wearing the Golden Jacket!" Taking her by the hand, he stared with mouth gaping open. "Dianna, you look lovely."

# ABOUT THE AUTHOR

Mr. Ercanbrack is a retired business owner. He worked in the oil and gas business for forty years. He has a great interest in writing and literature. Having written many poems and short stories, none of which were published. His inspiration in writing this book comes from his love of the stories from the Book of Mormon. This is Mr. Ercanbrack's first published book. He hopes to have many more in the years to come, writing stories that teach good morals and values for today's readers. His interests are his family, writing, and trying to make the world a better place one person at a time.

CPSIA information can be obtained
at www.ICGtesting.com
Printed in the USA
BVHW032342130421
604814BV00012B/1500/J

9 781636 921143